ERIN ENTRADA KELLY

Blackbird Fly

Greenwillow Books
An Imprint of HarperCollinsPublishers

Blackbird Fly

Text copyright © 2015 by Erin Entrada Kelly

The text of this book is set in Garamond.

Book design by Sylvie Le Floc'h

Interior illustrations by Betsy Peterschmidt

Library of Congress Cataloging-in-Publication Data

Kelly, Erin Entrada.

Blackbird fly / by Erin Entrada Kelly.

pages cm

"Greenwillow Books."

Summary: Bullied at school, eighth-grader Apple, a Filipino American who loves the music of the Beatles, decides to change her life by learning how to play the guitar.

ISBN 978-0-06-223861-0 (hardback)

[1. Bullying—Fiction. 2. Music—Fiction. 3. Guitar—Fiction. 4. Filipino Americans—Fiction. 5. Middle schools—Fiction. 6. Schools—Fiction.] I. Title.

PZ7.1.K45Bl 2015 [Fic]—dc23 2014029444

15 16 17 18 19 CG/RRDH 10 9 8 7 6 5 4 3 2 1

First Edition

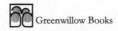 Greenwillow Books

To my parents,

Virgilia Sy Entrada and Dennis Ray Kelly

Contents

1. The Day It Snowed

2nd-Favorite Song 4 Now:
"Sunshine Life for Me"

On the day we moved to America, it snowed in Chapel Spring, Louisiana, for the first time in twenty years. My mother said it was a sign that the seasons of our lives were changing. Even though I was only four years old, I can still remember how she hugged me close and said we had something wonderful to look forward to: a life as real Americans.

When you start a new life, you're supposed to

get rid of everything from your old one—according to my mom, at least—so on the day it snowed, my mom had nothing from the Philippines except for her Catholic Bible and a picture of her grandmother. I had an old postcard and a Beatles cassette tape. *Abbey Road*, to be exact. My father had written his name on it in black marker a long, long time ago. *H. Yengko*, it said. Some of the letters had rubbed off, but his name was as clear as ever to me. I grabbed the tape quickly before we left our *barangay*, because it was the only thing that would fit in my pocket.

For a long time I couldn't listen to the tape because I didn't have a tape player, but last year I found one for ten cents at a garage sale and then I heard the tape for the first time. I could tell that my dad listened to it a lot, because the tape was cracked and the names of the songs were faded, but I understood right away why he wore it down. Once you listen to the Beatles, you can't go back. They're the best rock band that's ever lived, in my opinion.

George Harrison is my favorite Beatle. He mostly played lead guitar, but he also sang and wrote songs.

If I could ask my dad any question, I would ask him who his favorite Beatle was. I wish I could ask my mom if she knows, but she doesn't like when I mention my father, and she especially doesn't like when I talk about music. I think my mom is the only person in the world who doesn't have a favorite song. My all-time favorite song is "Blackbird"—by the Beatles, of course—but my second-favorite song for now is "Sunshine Life for Me," written by George and performed by my third-favorite Beatle, Ringo Starr.

My mom may not have a favorite song, but she has favorite stories. One of them is about the day we arrived in America. The day it snowed. That's the story she told the morning of Alyssa Tate's party, as she stirred a pot of sizzling garlic fried rice and adjusted her apron. It was the white one with *Mabuhay Philippines!* written on it in fat, red letters. I always thought it was funny how she couldn't wait to become American, but once we lived in America, she surrounded herself with things from back home. We have a Santo Niño in our curio cabinet, *pancit* and chicken adobo in our refrigerator, and that apron. Stupid apron.

She tells the story of how we came here after my father died, but she never says "after your father died." Instead she says "after everything that happened."

It hadn't even snowed a full inch when we got to Chapel Spring that day, but the ice crunched under our feet as my mother's best friend, Lita, led us to our yellow two-bedroom house on Oak Park Drive. Since it was cold and there was snow on the ground, I asked if that meant Santa was coming.

"Remember that, Apple? Remember?" My mother smiled into her pot of rice. The smell of garlic filled the whole house.

I moved lettuce around in my bowl but didn't say anything. I looked at the seven baby carrots in my salad. My mother knows I don't eat them anymore, but she keeps feeding them to me anyway.

I remember the day she's talking about. I remember how my new coat felt heavy and the new house smelled weird. I remember asking about Santa, missing the water of the ocean, and hearing Lita tell me how lucky I was.

I stabbed the carrots one by one with my fork and set them aside on a napkin next to my plate. The oil from the salad dressing soaked through and onto the table, because my mother buys the cheapest brand of napkins. The cheapest brand of everything.

She eyed the napkin. "I thought carrots were your favorite." She pointed at me with her spoon. "Carrots make good eyes, you know."

I've been having the same carrot conversation with her for five years, but my mother and I are like a merry-go-round when it comes to conversations. We've run out of new things to talk about, so instead we talk about the same things over and over, like our first day in America and how carrots used to be my favorite thing to eat.

Back when I still believed in carrots, Lita told me

she'd read a story in a magazine about a model whose face turned orange because she ate carrots all day. That's when my mother told me to be careful and to not eat too many.

"You used to eat lots of carrots," she said. "I waited on you to turn orange."

Here's a secret though: Carrots were never really my favorite. I hated how their gristly skin snapped between my teeth and how they tasted not-really-sweet and not-really-bitter, but I would eat them until I was full, because when I was seven years old my mother told me they "made good eyes." I'd eat them by the bag, expecting my eyes to turn blue, but they stayed slanted and dark with short, stubby eyelashes. Just like they are now.

I found out later that carrots were supposedly good for vision, not for color or shape, but who cares about that when you can get eyeglasses or contacts? Nothing fixes slanted eyes.

I watched the wet ring from the carrots expand on the napkin and listened to my mother hum Filipino love songs. It's strange to hear her hum, because there's nothing musical about her. I don't think she realizes she does it. If she did, she would stop.

"When we were at the mall yesterday, I saw a guitar for only twenty dollars," I said.

She stopped humming, her mouth a straight, tight line.

I speared a piece of sliced onion and let it dangle, then fall. "You said I could get one if I found one that was cheap enough."

My mother sighed. "School just started. You need to focus on schoolwork."

"I make honor roll every year."

"You're too old for toys."

"How am I going to be the next George Harrison or John Lennon if I don't have a guitar?"

"That's enough, *anak*."

"You said I could get one. You said that at the beginning of summer. It's almost October now." My chest felt hot.

She clicked off the stove and stirred the rice one final time. "Lunch is ready."

"I don't care about lunch," I said.

"*Ay*, Apple," she said, shaking her head. "You need to eat lunch."

We were back on the merry-go-round. Now she would tell me I needed to eat because she was a toothpick when she was a girl, and all the children teased her until she finally gained some weight. And then she'd say that even though you don't want to be too skinny, you don't want to be too fat either. You have to be somewhere in the middle, like her.

"You told me I could get a guitar," I said quickly.

Her jaw twitched the way it does when she's irritated, but I didn't care.

"I don't want to talk about this again, Apple. We've had this talk so many times. Save it for later."

This is what she always says, but later never comes. She just says this because she thinks I'll forget, but I won't forget. A famous songwriter needs a guitar. It's a necessity. George Harrison had one. Paul Simon, Norah Jones—they all have guitars.

"That's what you always say," I said.

"Ay, sus," she said. "Watch the mouth. You're getting too American."

I pushed back my chair.

"I'm not hungry," I said. "I'm going to ride my bike."

"With friends or by yourself?"

I pretended not to hear her and headed toward the back door, where I snatched my weekend backpack from the corner. My weekend backpack looks just like a school backpack, but instead of lame textbooks it's packed with a change of clothes, my red notebook, and bottled water. I used to keep *Abbey Road* in there too, but then I almost left my backpack on the bus, and if there's one place in the world you don't want to leave your prized possession, it's the bus.

"It's a shame you have no buddy-up system," my mother called from the kitchen. "It's not good for children to be going around by themselves all the time. In the Philippines none of the children played by themselves."

"This isn't the Philippines," I said, on my way out the door.

2. Dog-Eater

2FS4N: "Let It Be"

I climbed on my bike's faded banana seat and took off. My bike is pretty crappy, and the chain falls off sometimes. When it does, I have to lift up the back wheel and reset it. It's a big pain, but I have a special tool for it in my backpack. It doesn't help that Oak Park is full of cracked sidewalks. Sometimes I play songs in my head and swerve around the cracks in tune with the music, just to make it interesting.

Pretty soon sweat dribbled down my forehead and between my shoulder blades. There are lots of trees along the five blocks between my street and Alyssa Tate's, so the sun isn't that bad, but once I made a right onto Alyssa's street, the trees disappeared. The lack of trees makes it hard for me to hide my bike and change my shirt, but over the summer I found a perfect cluster of tall shrubs about four houses down from the Tates, so that's where I pulled over, parked my bike, and crouched to change out of my sweaty T-shirt and into the fresh one I always carry. I took a big swig of water, then came out from behind the shrubs with my old bike and bag still hidden.

There weren't any other bikes outside Alyssa's house, which meant the boys hadn't shown up yet. It was four weeks into the school year, and Alyssa always had a back-to-school party, but this year she invited only me, Gretchen Scott, and some of the boys from our grade. She said it was her mission to have a boyfriend all year, and she had her sights on Jake Bevans.

Alyssa's mother took me through the air-conditioned house and toward the back deck to meet up with the girls.

"I hope you didn't walk all the way from your house. It's a million degrees outside!" Mrs. Tate said. Her blond hair was piled on top of her head in a clip, and her eyes were round and blue. Very American. "If you needed a ride, I would have been happy to pick you up."

"It's okay. My mom dropped me off."

She glanced toward the front door and frowned. "Oh, was your mother outside? I would've liked to say hello."

"She was in a hurry."

Gretchen and Alyssa were on the back patio. Alyssa was sitting in the chair the way she did when she knew boys might be watching—with her legs crossed and her head tilted to the side. When we first became friends in fifth grade, she never cared how she looked when she sat. Back then we talked about how we were going to be a rock duo, with me on guitar and her on vocals. But later she changed her mind and said she wanted to be a Broadway star instead or a pop star like Britney Spears.

Now she mostly talked about boys.

"Hey, Apple," said Gretchen. Her hair was pulled into a ponytail, and her lips were covered in pink gloss.

"Hey," I said. I sat on the empty patio bench, pulled my legs to my chest, and rested my chin on my knees.

Alyssa grabbed a lock of her hair and twisted it around her finger. "The boys are on their way. I think Jake is bringing a bunch of people."

Five minutes later the back door opened and the boys wandered in, but it wasn't a bunch of people. It was just three: Jake Bevans, Lance Bosch, and Braden Tucker, each wearing a cap for a team in New York or Boston or Chicago, places that might as well be a million miles away. Braden was in my homeroom, but we hardly ever talked.

Jake sat in the seat next to Alyssa, and Lance sat next to Gretchen. Even though there was a big, empty space next to me on the bench, Braden sat on the arm of Jake's chair.

"Is there anyone else coming to this thing?" Braden asked.

"Maybe," said Alyssa.

Jake leaned away from Braden. "Go sit down somewhere. Get your butt out of my face."

Everyone laughed except for me and Braden.

Jake nudged him and nearly knocked him over. "Go."

"Suck it," said Braden.

"Dude, there's room on the bench, and I don't want your butt in my face," said Jake. He nudged him again; this time Braden slipped off the arm of the chair and stumbled a few steps. Everyone laughed. Braden thumped Jake on the back of the head, sat down, and said something to Jake that none of us could hear.

My heart thumped. I glanced at Alyssa and Gretchen, but they were busy looking at the boys with bright, light eyes.

"This sucks," said Braden. "I thought it was a party."

"It would be, if you would get out of my face," Jake said.

Alyssa giggled.

"Just let him sit there, Bevans, so he'll shut up," said Lance. He and Gretchen looked like they could be brother and sister. They both had the same light brown hair and light brown eyes. "What's the big deal?"

Jake motioned toward the vast space of wilderness next to me. "The big deal is, he's sitting next to me like a pansy, and there's all that space next to whatshername." He narrowed his eyes at me. "What's your name again? What is it, like, Banana or Orange or something?"

Jake Bevans does this act where he pretends he doesn't know who I am, even though we sat next to each other in third grade, spent half of fourth grade in a study group, and talked for an hour during a bus ride on a fifth-grade field trip. Back then he didn't have too many acts. He was just a skinny kid who kept to himself. Now he's one of the tallest guys in the class. He must've taken some kind of growth hormone when no one was paying attention.

"My name's Apple," I said. "Remember when we got stuck sitting together on that bus in fifth grade?"

Jake snorted. "Why would I remember something like that?"

"It was the trip where you threw up all over yourself." The words burst out of my mouth by themselves. I wasn't even trying to be mean, but I knew he remembered that bus ride.

The others laughed. Jake's face fell, flat and red.

"Aw, poor baby," Lance said, leaning back in his chair. "Did your mommy have to come pick you up?"

The girls and Braden laughed.

Jake glared at me.

"It wasn't a big deal," I said, even though it was a really big deal, because the driver had to pull over and we had to call Jake's mother and everything. We were a half hour late getting to the zoo because of it. "Everyone gets carsick sometimes. I know I do."

"I'm sure you get sick a lot because of all the dogs you eat," said Jake.

Every part of my body froze. The air left my lungs. I heard the comment again, even though he hadn't repeated it. *I'm sure you get sick a lot because of all the dogs you eat.*

"What are you talking about?" asked Alyssa.

"Chinese people eat dogs for dinner," said Jake. He glanced around. "You guys didn't know that? It doesn't even matter what breed. It's illegal to even keep them as pets in China."

Alyssa's eyes turned wide and round. She looked at me. "Is that true?"

"Apple isn't even Chinese," said Gretchen.

"It doesn't matter." Jake crossed his arms. "It's all Asian people, not just Chinese. They all eat dogs."

"Why?" Alyssa asked.

Jake shrugged. "I don't know. Ask Banana here."

Braden and Lance chuckled.

My whole body felt hot, like I'd suddenly developed a life-threatening fever.

Alyssa raised her eyebrows at me. "Apple, is this true? Do Chinese people eat dogs for dinner?"

"I'm not Chinese," I said.

Alyssa rolled her eyes as if to say, *We know, we know, but close enough.*

"She may not be Chinese, but I guarantee you don't wanna go to her house and ask her mom for hot dogs," Jake said. He put his fingers on the corners of his eyes and pulled them to make slits. "Would you-ah like-ah Chinese-tea with-ah you-ah hot-dahg?"

Braden covered his mouth with his fist in a fake

attempt to hide his laughter. Lance clapped his hands and leaned forward, saying, "That's so wrong, man," between his own laughing howls.

Jake looked directly at me and said, "There's more than one reason you wound up on the Dog Log."

Everything stopped. The laughter. My heart. Time. It was like Jake had thrown a grenade at all of us—a grenade that hit only me.

Alyssa's jaw dropped. She looked back and forth between me and Jake.

I prayed for a giant earthquake to crack open the ground and pull me down, deep into the earth. I wanted to bolt and run and hide forever.

"Apple's on the Dog Log?" asked Alyssa.

A swell rose from deep inside my chest.

Jake shrugged.

Gretchen looked at her hands.

Even Braden and Lance weren't saying anything.

"What number is she?" asked Alyssa.

"I don't know," mumbled Jake.

A few seconds passed—seconds that felt like a thousand lifetimes—before Gretchen finally broke the silence.

"Is anyone else coming over, Alyssa?" she asked.

"Yeah, is anyone else coming?" said Braden. He turned to Alyssa and pulled his cap down low. It cast a shadow on his face, hiding his pockmarks.

Lance stood up and walked to the cooler on the other end of the patio. "Yeah, Braden," he said. "Your mom."

Braden stole Lance's seat and smiled like he'd just won a victory. We all watched Lance walk back, waiting for the confrontation we knew was coming. Everyone was smiling—everyone but me. I pressed my lips together tight. It seemed like everyone had moved on from the Dog Log, except for Alyssa, who turned away every time I looked at her.

When he got back with his soda, Lance glared down at his seat and said, "Get up."

Braden smirked. "Make me."

Lance set down his soda and wrestled with Braden until the legs of the chair scraped against the concrete. Gretchen squealed and jumped up as they shoved their way in her direction.

"I told you to get out of my seat!" said Lance, his face red and laughing. He had Braden in a headlock.

Braden struggled. His cap fell off, exposing a hat-head of sandy-brown hair. He flailed his arms. "Don't make me sit next to the dog-eater!" he hollered.

Jake thought it was so hysterical, he almost fell out of his chair. I wanted to stand up and tell all of them about what he'd been like on that bus ride—how he looked at me with big, scared eyes after he'd gotten sick and how I had to find his cell phone in his backpack, the one his mom gave him for emergencies, and how I walked to the front of the bus to tell the teacher what happened. I wanted to tell them that I whispered it to her so he wouldn't be embarrassed and that I stood a certain way in the aisle so the other kids wouldn't see the mess he'd made.

"Sit next to her—she might eat your little pup!" Jake hollered.

Alyssa looked straight at me, so I smiled and tried to laugh to show that none of it bothered me, but I couldn't really laugh, because an enormous lump had formed in my throat. I swallowed it away and listened to the sound of the blood rushing in my ears—*tha-thump, tha-thump, tha-thump.*

Gretchen moved next to me in a puff of vanilla perfume and Pantene shampoo.

"You can have my seat, Lance," she said.

Finally Lance sat back in his seat, and Braden sat where Gretchen had been. Everyone talked about how the school year was going, the homerooms everyone was in, the teachers they liked and hated. Everyone agreed that Mr. Zervanos—or Mr. Z, as we all called him—was their favorite teacher. Then Gretchen and Alyssa talked about Tuesday's swing-choir auditions, because Mr. Z was in charge of them.

I wanted to try out for swing choir, but my mom

wouldn't let me, so usually when the subject came up I felt a twinge of jealousy, but right now all I saw were the words *Dog Log* in my head, like a bright neon light.

"Swing choir?" Jake scrunched his nose. "What is that anyway?"

"It's just for our grade," Gretchen explained. "It's a performance group that puts on shows, like musicals and stuff."

"That sounds like the gayest club in school," said Jake.

Alyssa stood up. "Let's go to the woods," she said, nodding toward the trees that lined the Tates' unfenced backyard. Everyone else stood up too—first Jake and Alyssa, then Lance and Gretchen and, slowly, Braden and me.

Alyssa looked at me the same way my fourth-grade reading teacher used to when I got answers wrong.

"You need to stay here, Apple," she said. "Just in case my mom comes out."

Lance smacked Braden on the back and said, "You stay here too. Keep her company."

"No way," said Braden. "I'm not hangin' out on some sorry-ass porch waiting for Alyssa's mom just so you retards can make out in the woods."

Jake leaned over and whispered something to Braden. They both laughed.

My feet felt like two big blocks of cement.

"What am I supposed to say if she comes out?" I asked.

Alyssa grabbed Jake's hand. Backing away, she said, "Just tell her we went to Claire Hathaway's house."

"Ooh, Claire Hathaway!" said Braden. "I wouldn't mind taking her for a walk in the woods."

Claire Hathaway was a cheerleader with soft, red hair and big, green eyes. She lived down the road.

I watched them cross the yard. Gretchen looked back once. Alyssa did too. She waved, but I didn't wave back. Once they were finally in the trees, I stepped off the porch and walked around the Tates' house and down the sidewalk until I reached my shrub. I put on my backpack and got on my bike. I pedaled fast, then faster. My bike chain rattled, but I didn't care. I didn't even ride around the cracks in the sidewalk— the ones that looked like they'd been pushed up from the center of the earth—I just kept pedaling and pedaling until the back of my neck burned with heat.

The bike chain broke as soon as I pulled up to my back porch. I hopped off and let my bike fall to the grass in a loud *clank*.

When I came through the door, my mom looked up at me from the sofa, where she was reading a fashion magazine. She smiled and blinked at me. I thought about Jake and his Chinese eye slits. I thought about the Dog Log.

"No fun being alone, huh?" she said.

I went straight to my room, shut the door, and sat on my bed. I closed my eyes tight and imagined myself walking down the hallway and into the living room. I imagined myself standing in front of my mother and looking into her dark, slanted eyes.

"Dog-eater," I said.

3. None of the Above

2FS4N: "For No One"

At the beginning of every school year at Chapel Spring Middle, a group of guys comes up with a list of the ten ugliest girls. They call it the Dog Log. The names on the list are half mystery and half public. Heleena Moffett and Martha Leibovitz were on it every year. At the beginning of school last year, Alyssa and I had talked about the Dog Log and what we would do if we were ever on it.

"I would transfer schools," Alyssa had said. She was on the swing of her front porch with one leg dangling down. We were both eating bologna sandwiches—no mustard, lots of mayo, with the crusts taken off the bread. "I would never show my face at school again."

"You don't have to worry," I'd told her. "You would never wind up on it anyway. You're too pretty."

"I wouldn't end up on it because no one even knows who I am," she'd said.

I told her she was lucky. She was new, which meant she could be anyone she wanted. She could reinvent herself completely. After that she was quiet for a while. I waited for her to tell me that I was too pretty for the Dog Log too, but she didn't.

I turned on the Beatles' *White Album*, collapsed on my bed with my backpack still on my shoulders, stared at the ceiling, and listened to "Blackbird." I closed my eyes and imagined I was flying away, just like the bird in the song. I imagined it was a thousand years in the future and the Dog Log didn't matter. But then I opened my eyes and it *did* matter. My cheeks were wet, and my eyes burned. I slipped off my backpack and went to my mirror to see what a girl who is considered one of the ugliest girls in school looks like.

My head was round and red when I was born. That's why I'm called Apple. My real name is Analyn Pearl Yengko, but in the Philippines no one calls you by your real name. Filipinos are known for giving funny nicknames, some of which don't make any sense. My mother's name is Amihan, but everyone calls her Glo.

My eyes: slanted and dark. Not American.

My hair: black, straight, and thick, but not silky.

My body: *palito*. Too skinny, with no curves anywhere.

Everything about me was Filipino. Everything about me said DOG-EATER and DOG LOG. Even my house. My mother was in the kitchen again, heating up leftover *pancit* for dinner. I could smell it.

I went down the hall with my eyes still burning. My mother was pulling the bowl of noodles out of the microwave. I opened the refrigerator to get a soda— the generic brand of Coke that just said *Cola* on the side.

"Can't we ever eat something normal?" I asked.

"What you mean?"

"Can't we just order a pizza? Why do we always have to eat stuff like this?" I shut the fridge and motioned to the *pancit*.

My mother raised her eyebrows and looked down at the noodles. "You always eat *pancit*." She put the bowl on the counter and pulled plates out of the cabinet. "Pizza is too expensive and isn't good for you. That's why American children are so fat—they're always eating pizza. If I spent all my money on pizza like Americans do, I'd have none left to send back home."

She was always sending money back home. That's

why she bought the cheapest brand of everything.
That's why I never got name-brand jeans like Alyssa
did or designer backpacks like Gretchen had.

"If you care about back home so much, why did
we come here?" I mumbled.

But my mother didn't hear me.

And even though the *pancit* smelled just like it
always did, and I wanted to eat a bowlful, I said, "I
don't want any of that stuff. It stinks, and it's gross."

She sighed and turned around to face me. "*Ay, sus.*
What's wrong with you today, Apple?"

"I don't want to be called Apple anymore." The
can of cola felt like a cold, heavy brick. I didn't even
really want to drink it. I don't even know why I'd come
into the kitchen. "I want to go by my real name."

A bunch of lines crinkled across my mother's
forehead. "Why? Nothing's wrong with your name.
It's a good name."

"It's not even a name," I said. My chest ached. I
wished I could throw the drink at my mother.

My mother frowned. "Your father gave you that nickname."

I thought of my father's name written in black marker on *Abbey Road*. When you write your name on something, it means it's really important to you, so it must have been one of his most prized possessions. I always thought that meant he was creative and smart. But if he was so creative and smart, why did he give me such a stupid nickname? Did he ever think about how it would make *me* feel? Did he ever think about how *my* name would look when I had to write it on things?

I swallowed. "I don't care." And why should I? The only pieces of information I had about my father besides the tape were a few fuzzy memories and a postcard from our island in the Philippines, and that's not really information; it's just a picture of where we lived. There aren't even any people in the picture. Just a white sandy beach and blue water. My mother's always saying that she moved us to America to have a better life, and I still haven't figured out how Chapel Spring, Louisiana, is better than a white sandy beach. When we first moved here, I'd stare at the postcard and imagine my mother and father holding hands and standing with their feet in the water, but now I keep it in my nightstand under a pile of old notebooks. What's the point?

My mother frowned. "You don't care?"

"No."

"What would your father say?"

I could see the remembering in her eyes—about how I used to ask her to tell me the story of the day I was born, and even though I felt a tug at the remembering look, I didn't care. I liked that she was frowning. She needed to frown. It was her fault I was on the Dog Log—she's the one who moved me here; she's the one who was really Filipino.

"He's dead, remember?" I said. The coldness of the soda can numbed my fingers. "And you're not the one who has to go to school with a stupid name like Apple."

The words came out of my mouth, one after the other. The air suddenly became heavy.

"Okay, *Analyn*," my mother said, and she turned around to put my serving of *pancit* back into its leftover container.

I went to my room and pushed everything away—my mother's remembering look, my father giving me a funny nickname in some village on the other side of the world, the way I felt standing on Alyssa's porch, the words *dog-eater* and *Chinese* and *Dog Log*. I stared at my reflection in the bedroom mirror again and listened to the Beatles sing "Don't Pass Me By."

"Hello," I said. "My name is Analyn Yengko." *Analyn. Analyn. Analyn. A-n-a-l-y-n-Y-e-n-g-k-o.*

All the crying had turned my eyes pink.

Just call me Analyn.

"My name is Analyn Yengko," said the girl in the mirror.

I pulled up my hair into a ponytail like Gretchen's.

Analyn Yengko: popular and funny. Analyn Yengko: the prettiest girl in school. Analyn Yengko: lots of friends and boyfriends. Analyn Yengko: does not eat dogs for dinner.

"Good-bye, Apple," I said. "Hello, Analyn."

But what was the point of a new name when everyone knows who you really are?

I was Apple Yengko: none of the above. And everyone knew it, including me.

4. Still Almost Okay

2FS4N: "Across the Universe"

In homeroom on Monday, I wondered how many people knew that I was on the Dog Log. It felt like everyone knew, like I was wearing a big sandwich board that said *Ugly*. I watched Claire Hathaway and her friends laughing and catching up on their weekends. None of them were on the list, that was for sure. I watched Claire arrange her books and say something to Caleb Robinson sitting next to her, and

I thought about Jake, Lance, and Braden wanting to take a walk with her in the woods, and even though the thought of kissing Braden Tucker's chapped lips was the most disgusting thing I could imagine, I would have done anything to trade places with Claire Hathaway right then and there. Let Claire have slanty eyes and dark skin and go home to *pancit* and garlic. I'll be the white American cheerleader.

When Mr. Ted stood up at the podium, I turned away from Claire and focused on him instead. That was much easier, because there are only a few things worse than being the only dog-eater at Chapel Spring Middle School, and one of them was being Ted Stanley, the math teacher.

I believe that everyone on Earth has at least three interesting facts about them. One of Mr. Ted's IFs is that he wore the same outfit—or at least the same idea of an outfit—every single day. Flower-print button-up shirt, like he was leaving for a trip to Hawaii that afternoon. Faded khaki pants with pleats that puffed up front, so it looked like he was carrying a balloon. Black-rimmed eyeglasses. Occasionally mismatched socks.

On the first day of school in August, he told us to call him Mr. Ted instead of Mr. Stanley. He said Mr. Stanley was "just too formal," and we could "all show respect by using our first names." Then he lifted his arm to write *MR. TED* in big, block letters on the board, and we all saw rings of sweat on the flower-print of his armpits. Braden was the first to notice. He snorted and snickered behind me.

One of Braden's three IFs: He loved practical jokes but never the fun kind.

That day Braden called Mr. Ted "Sweaty Teddy" under his breath, and Danica Landry laughed. That was all Braden needed. From then on it was Sweaty Teddy this and Sweaty Teddy that. It'd been Sweaty Teddy since day one, and Danica still giggled.

Mr. Ted didn't just sweat that first day either. He

sweated the day after that and the day after that. What made it worse was that he was a really nice teacher, and when people like Braden answered questions correctly and called him Mr. Ted with a big, fake smile, I could tell that he felt like we really were a team showing mutual respect to one another. I try to send Mr. Ted mental mind waves. *Please, Mr. Ted, change your shirt or use some deodorant so that they'll quit calling you Sweaty Teddy.* But I knew that once he was Sweaty Teddy, he was stuck with it, even if he wore fresh shirts and smelled like honey for the rest of the school year. Just like I was stuck being Apple.

Mr. Ted and his big display of red and orange flowers knocked on the podium three times, the way he always did when it was time to "quiet down, please, quiet down."

"I am pleased that you are all in my homeroom, because that means I get the pleasure of sharing with you the destination of this year's excursion." Another of Mr. Ted's IFs: He liked to change plain words into fancier ones. Like saying *excursion* instead of *field trip*. He cleared his throat. "The destination of this year's voyage, ladies and gentlemen, is . . ." He raised up his arms, palms out for emphasis, and smiled slyly, like he was sharing a big secret with a bunch of friends. We all stared back at him and the beginnings of his sweat rings. "New Orleans."

Whoops and hollers all around.

Mr. Ted's smile got bigger and bigger, like our excitement was contagious and spreading across his face.

"New Orleans is three hours away, so it'll be a long journey. Be sure to get your parents' permission and ask them to sign up if they want to chaperone." Mr. Ted laid a stack of permission slips on Claire's desk. Claire sat in the first desk of the first row, and Mr. Ted always gave her the papers to pass out. I think that's why she sat there.

She immediately popped up with the permission slips tucked in the crook of her arm, then licked her index finger to pass them out. She did this at the head of every row. She was very serious about passing out papers. I didn't really like the idea of having a permission slip smeared with a spitty finger, but I didn't have much choice.

The permission slip outlined our agenda for the day: aquarium, lunch, planetarium, museum. The trip was in eight weeks, just before Thanksgiving break. Mr. Ted went over every detail piece by piece, but no one was really listening. Everyone was blabbing about how lucky we were that we didn't get stuck with a boring trip to the state capitol. I was busy thinking about the Dog Log and tearing the chaperone sign-up portion from the bottom of the paper so I could get rid of it.

After the bell, I made my way to Gretchen's locker. Gretchen and Alyssa looked like they were deep in conversation. Gretchen was shoving textbooks into her designer backpack and nodding at Alyssa's every other word. Alyssa talked a million miles a minute. When I walked up, she stopped talking midsentence.

"What *happened* to you Saturday?" she asked. "We got back, and you were gone."

"I had to get home. What'd you guys do anyway?"

Alyssa smiled and tilted her head. "Things . . ."

"So Jake kissed you?" I asked, trying hard to not show what I was really thinking, which was that I would rather lick one of Mr. Ted's shirts than kiss Jake Bevans.

Not that he would make out with me anyway.

"More like *she* kissed *him*," Gretchen said.

Alyssa sighed. Cool and casual. "Well, sometimes you just can't wait for the other person to make a move."

Alyssa had kissed one boy over the summer, so now she was pretending like she was some kind of professional seductress. Gretchen had a boyfriend at the beach and they kissed three times, but Alyssa pretends that doesn't really count—although I'm not sure why.

"You're such a vixen," said Gretchen. They giggled.

I was about to ask what they thought about the field trip when I looked over Alyssa's shoulder and saw Heleena Moffett coming our way. She walked slowly, the way she always did—not really swinging her arms, not really looking around. Just rolling down the hall like an enormous beach ball. She probably weighed more than me, Gretchen, and Alyssa combined. Everyone stepped out of her way instinctively. She reminded me of a giant fish swimming through a school of minnows. And she always swam alone.

I bumped Gretchen's hip lightly. "Hurry up, slowpoke."

"What's the big rush?" asked Alyssa.

"Almost ready," Gretchen said. She slipped on her backpack, pulled out a tube of lipstick from the little shelf in her locker, and put some on. Her lips brightened up.

"Can I have some of that?" I asked.

Gretchen looked surprised but smiled. "Sure," she said, handing it to me.

Alyssa crossed her arms and leaned against the locker next to Gretchen's, which belonged to Heleena. "It's a little late for that now," she said.

"What do you mean?" I asked, looking into Gretchen's locker mirror as I applied the lipstick.

"You're already on *the list*. You should've been doing that last year."

I handed the lipstick to Gretchen. I felt like I'd been socked in the gut. I also felt completely ridiculous.

"Alyssa!" Gretchen said. "That was a little harsh, don't you think?"

Alyssa looked away. "Sorry, Apple. I woke up in a bad mood, that's all. And I'm so pissed off that you're on that list. It's, like, so wrong."

I rubbed my lips together. Suddenly they felt like the brightest things in the world.

Gretchen closed her locker. "Wait a minute—ohmygod. Hold everything. My purse. It's not here." She reopened her locker and shuffled through her neatly stacked books as if her pink studded bag could be flattened between them.

One of Gretchen's IFs: She loses her purse about once a week. Sometimes she finds it right away. Other times she has to retrace her steps until she discovers it in the girls' bathroom or under the bleachers in the gym. I groaned.

Gretchen found her purse, but just before she closed her locker again, Heleena tapped Alyssa's shoulder. *Tap-tap-tap.* Alyssa's ponytail whipped around. I smelled coconut.

"Yes?" said Alyssa. Smooth like butter.

Heleena had a tiny voice. She's had the same tiny voice since second grade. It was the only tiny thing about her.

"Can I get to my locker, please?" she asked.

Alyssa blocked Heleena's locker 80 percent of the time. At first I didn't think it was on purpose, but now I'm not so sure.

"Oh, I'm sorry." Alyssa put her hand to her chest.

"I would have moved, but I didn't see you coming."

Alyssa shifted to the side to get out of Heleena's way, but she didn't move far enough. She never did. Heleena had to say excuse me two more times.

"Sorry again for getting in your way," said Alyssa as we headed down the hall. "Blame Gretchen. She takes forever." She rolled her eyes in a big display that said, *You know how best friends can be.*

Heleena turned the dial on her locker without saying anything.

"I always try to be nice to her, because I know she doesn't have any friends, but god, could she be more disgusting?" said Alyssa, under her breath. "She needs some serious help. That's not even *healthy*. I heard she even has lunch in the library, because no one can stand to watch her eat. Or maybe it's just because she has no friends." Alyssa turned to me. "You may be on *the list*, Apple, but it could be worse. At least you aren't Big-leena Moffett." She paused. "Unless . . ."

"Unless what?" I said. The socked-gut feeling was

still there. I wouldn't have been surprised to lift up my shirt and see a big bruise.

"Unless you're above Heleena on the list," said Alyssa. She frowned.

Gretchen rolled her eyes. "That's not possible." She looked at me and said again: "That's not possible, Apple. And the list is stupid anyway. Who cares?"

But we all knew that everyone cared.

"I've got to find out what number you are," said Alyssa. She smiled and put her hand on my shoulder. "For your sake. Wouldn't you like to know? I mean, if you're, like, eighth, that's not so bad, is it? That's still almost okay."

"Still almost okay for what?" I asked.

But she didn't answer.

5. Hello, Good-bye

2FS4N: "Hello, Goodbye"

Gretchen, Alyssa, and I settled in our usual spots under the giant oak tree for lunch and waited for a "big announcement" from Alyssa. She loved to make big announcements. It was one of her IFs. She made one almost every day.

She inhaled sharply, like she was about to tell us that she had terminal cancer.

"I don't think I'm going to try out for swing

choir tomorrow," she said.

Gretchen gasped—her usual reaction. I opened my bag of chips.

"You have to!" said Gretchen. "Who will I hang out with? Besides, you're the best one."

Alyssa nodded as if to say, *I know, I know.* "I'm just not sure I can do everything." She opened her bag of Funyuns. "I'm doing community theater in the spring, and I've got dance class once a week."

"You *have* to, Alyssa," Gretchen said. "You *have* to."

Alyssa nodded again. *I know, I know.* "I'll think about it. I'll decide by tomorrow."

"Does this have anything to do with what Jake said?" I asked, popping the top on my soda. "About swing choir being the gayest club in school?"

"As if I care what he says," she said. "I do what I want. I just think it might be too much for my schedule. You know how busy I am. It's a good thing I didn't join the cheerleading squad."

The truth is, she didn't *make* the cheerleading squad.

I took a big swig of soda and decided to change the subject. The less we talked about Jake Bevans and his friends, the better.

"What do you guys think about the field trip?" I asked. I was looking at Gretchen, but Alyssa answered.

"Great!" she said. "I already have ideas on what I'm gonna wear. Then again, I might get my mom to buy something new. We have, like, an eternity before we even leave." Suddenly her face lit up. Another announcement. "Speaking of new outfits, guess what else I found out today?"

We looked at her, waiting.

"We get to wear Halloween costumes to the fall dance this year," she said. "It's going to be *a-may-zing*. We need to discuss costume concepts."

Gretchen shoved a handful of Skittles into her mouth. "I was gonna be a zombie bride for Halloween."

"Don't you think we're too old for that sort of thing?" said Alyssa.

I turned to Gretchen. "I like the zombie bride idea."

"Thanks," she said. "What about you, Apple? What's your costume concept?"

"Apple isn't going to the dance," said Alyssa, before I could answer. She turned to me with wide eyes. "Are you?"

"I don't know. I was thinking about it," I said. "Why wouldn't I?"

"Last year you said dances were lame."

I didn't tell Alyssa that the reason I'd said that was because they both got brand-new outfits and I knew my mom would never get me one, which meant I'd have to wear something they'd already seen at school. But a Halloween party was another story—I could make my own costume.

"So are you saying you changed your mind?" said Alyssa.

"I don't know," I said. "It depends."

"Well, I know I'm going for sure. And I have a feeling Jake will ask me."

"I'll probably go with Lance." Gretchen crumpled up her empty Skittles bag and put it in her pocket. She liked to put her junk-food trash in her pockets instead of walking ten feet to the trash can. One of her IFs.

"Why do we need dates?" I asked. "Nobody brought dates last year."

Alyssa sighed as if I were the dumbest person on Earth. "Things are different this year. Everyone's gonna have a date. Well, except maybe Big-leena." She snickered.

I scanned the lunch crowd for date possibilities of my own, but I saw only the same faces I'd seen since elementary school, and none of them would want to go with a girl on the Dog Log. Who could blame them? I saw the neon sign again—DOG LOG, DOG LOG, DOG LOG—and felt the corners of my eyes moisten, so I blinked and blinked and then pretended I had an eyelash caught in my eye. When I finally looked up, I saw an unfamiliar head of messy brown hair by the vending machines. It was a boy I'd never seen before. Even though he was standing in the crowd, he wasn't part of it. He was leaning against the wall, reading a book.

"Who's that?" I asked, pointing.

"I have no idea," said Alyssa. She squinted at him. "I don't remember hearing anything about a new student."

"Me neither," Gretchen and I said at the same time.

"What's he doing?" asked Gretchen. "Is he *reading a book* by the vending machines?"

Not many kids read books during lunch, but there he was. He looked really into it too. I wondered what the book was about.

"It's probably because he doesn't have anyone to talk to," Alyssa concluded. She stood up and brushed the grass off her bottom. Gretchen and I did the same.

"Are we going to talk to him?" I asked.

"Sure, why not?"

His pants were too long, so the cuffs curled under his dirty sneakers. I noticed he was wearing Vans, which is my second-favorite brand of sneaker after Chuck Taylors. You can tell a lot about someone by their sneakers. Alyssa used to tell me that I needed to wear different shoes, since my black Chucks are all worn down. She suggested I wear sandals like she and Gretchen did, but why would I wear sandals when I can wear comfortable shoes? Then again, maybe if I'd listened, I wouldn't be one of the ugliest girls in school.

The new boy's hair was long, and it hung in his eyes in a way that made me want to brush it away. The book he was reading was thick. He scrunched his eyebrows as he read it, the same way my mom does when she's playing cards.

"Hey," said Alyssa.

He didn't see us—or maybe he didn't hear us—so he kept right on reading.

"Hey," said Alyssa again, louder. She put her hand on her hip.

He looked up.

"Hey," he said, glancing quickly at all three of us before going back to his book.

"Uh . . . hello?" said Alyssa.

He looked up again. "Hello." Then back to reading.

Alyssa looked at Gretchen and rolled her eyes. "Excuse me," she said. She put her hand over his book. "Are you new here?"

Finally he lowered his book. He looked completely irritated. I tried to see what he was reading, but all I could tell was that it was from the school library.

"Yeah, I'm new here," he said. His hair hung all around his face. When he blinked, some of the strands caught on his eyelashes.

"We wanted to introduce ourselves," said Alyssa.

"Okay." He blew his hair out of his eyes.

The four of us stood there for a while in silence.

"So go ahead," he said.

Alyssa had both hands on her hips now. "Ugh! Never mind." She turned around and walked off with Gretchen close behind. I introduced myself as Analyn before I followed too, a bit slower.

"Is that one word or two?" he asked. "Like Anna, and then Lynn?"

I turned around.

"No. Like A-N-A-L-Y-N."

"Cool," he said, nodding. "My name's Evan Temple. I just moved here from California."

A lot of really good songwriters live in California, like Matt Costa and Eleisha Eagle, so I thought about asking what music he liked, but instead I asked what book he was reading.

"*The Silmarillion,*" he said. He held it up so I could see the cover. It was by J. R. R. Tolkien. "It's the same guy who wrote *The Lord of the Rings.*"

"I love that movie," I said.

"You should read the book."

Alyssa called out, "Apple!" and motioned for me to come over. She glared at me like I was a traitor as I walked back to the oak tree.

"His name is Evan Temple," I said. "He's from California."

"Evan Temple?" Alyssa crinkled her nose. "What kind of stupid name is that?"

About as stupid as Apple, I thought.

The three of us glanced back at the new guy. He was reading again, but just before I looked away, I thought I saw him glance at me. I couldn't be sure though.

Alyssa talked about what a jerk the new guy was until the bell rang and Gretchen announced that she couldn't find her purse. While she and Alyssa looked for it, I turned back to the vending machines, but he'd already disappeared.

6. The Dog Log

2FS4N: "Act Naturally"

The Dog Log isn't actually written down. It's spread, guy to guy, until any guy who is "in the know" knows. It's a good thing for me it's not on paper, I guess, but that doesn't make it any less of a Dog Log.

The reason it's not written down is because, a few years ago, a bunch of boys got in big trouble for passing it around at school. They even got suspended. So, the next year, they just made it an unofficial-official list. That's what makes it a little mysterious.

The only thing worse than being on the Dog Log is being one of the top five on the Dog Log. Part of me wanted to know what my ranking was, and part of me wanted to die without ever knowing. Or just die, period. Alyssa was determined to figure it out though. As soon as she got home from school, she called to let me know that Jake had spilled everything.

When the call came in, I was sitting on the floor of my room, listening to *Abbey Road* and tapping my pencil on my social studies book in rhythm. I never played my dad's tape anymore, because it was in such bad shape, but I had the album downloaded on my laptop, along with *Sgt. Pepper's Lonely Hearts Club Band*, *Magical Mystery Tour*, *The White Album*, and *All Things Must Pass*, which is the first album George Harrison released after the group broke up.

Sometimes it feels like the Beatles are the soundtrack to my life. Sometimes it feels like music is the only thing that saves me, especially in moments like this, when my so-called best friend is ready to tell me how ugly I am.

"I know what number you are," she said. Her voice was serious. Too serious.

I dropped my pencil and moved to my bed. When you're about to hear bad news, it's nice to know you have a soft place to fall.

"I don't care," I said, even though my heart was beating so loudly, I was certain Alyssa could hear it. "Gretchen's right. It's stupid."

"The list is, like, really superficial," she said. "But don't you want to know what number you are? That way we can figure out how to get you off the list altogether."

"If it's superficial, who cares?" I said.

Alyssa sighed. "Do you really want to go to high school as one of the Dog Log girls? Think about it."

The Dog Log may not be written down, but it's impossible to erase. I knew the names of some of the

Dog Log girls who were in eighth grade when I was in fifth. Amanda McNally. Kim Achee. Bonnie Nyberg. I can't really remember what they looked like, but I remember their names.

Just like people would remember Apple Yengko.

"It doesn't matter," I said, but my voice sounded small and tiny, like Heleena's.

"Yes, it does. We're talking about tiers here, Apple."

Alyssa believes that every school is divided into tiers. The most popular people—the Claires, Jakes, Lances, and others—are on the first tier. They are the ones who always get invited, get nominated for this and that, and never in a million years would end up on any dog list. Alyssa thinks that we are somewhere between the second and third tier. She said that she had been headed for the fourth tier before she left Colorado, which was "a fate worse than anything," because there are no more than four tiers. Once you get below that, you join people like Heleena.

"We don't want to start the year on the wrong tier," Alyssa said.

"We?"

"You know what I mean."

I pressed my lips together, fell back on the bed, and put a pillow over my face. "Okay," I said, my voice muffled. "What number?"

Please let it be ten. Please let it be ten. Please let it be ten.

I would give anything for it to be ten.

Anything.

Just let it be ten.

Alyssa cleared her throat.

"Three," she said.

Three?

I opened my mouth to say a million things—*How could it be three? Am I really that ugly? I know I don't look like anyone else, but am I really* three*? Third-ugliest girl in middle school?* Third?—but nothing came out. My face suddenly started sweating under the heat of the pillow.

One. Two. Three.

I swallowed. A well of tears crushed my chest.

"Hello?" said Alyssa. "Did you hear me? I said you were—"

"Yes. I heard you." Three. I heard you. "Who are the others?"

"Heleena Moffett is first, of course. Then Dana Duttons." Dana Duttons was in the special-needs class. One time last year, she dropped her binder in the hall and all her papers flew out of it. Another girl and I helped her pick them all up. She said thank you but never looked up from the floor. That was the only time I've ever talked to Dana Duttons, and we hadn't really talked, but every time I've seen her, she's wearing something purple—a purple shirt, purple pants, purple bow, whatever. Purple has got to be her favorite color.

Dana Duttons on the Dog Log. She probably didn't even know what the Dog Log was, which made me feel even worse that she was on it.

Alyssa continued: "Fourth is Martha Leibovitz. Then—"

"Never mind," I said. "I don't want to hear the rest." I couldn't listen anymore. I suddenly felt terrible for even talking about the Dog Log—almost as bad as I felt about being on it. Maybe it's because I was on the list. Maybe it's because I was thinking about Dana Duttons. Whatever it was, I needed to get off the phone ASAP.

"I gotta go," I said, and before Alyssa could say anything, I hung up, tossed the phone off the bed, and pressed the pillow to my face again.

I imagined Jake Bevans and his friends sitting around talking about me and Dana Duttons and Heleena Moffett. I could already guess what words they used to describe Dana and Heleena. I wondered what words they used when they talked about me. Did they say *ugly*? Did they say *slanted eyes*? Did they say *flat nose* or *round face*? Did they say *dog-eater*? Did they laugh?

I thought about Alyssa and Jake. I thought about how I would never want to speak to Jake if he put a friend of mine on some ugly list, yet Alyssa blabbed to him long enough to get all ten names.

My face was wet before I even realized I was crying, and even though the pillow got soaked and made my skin itch, I didn't move. I imagined myself floating far away, not just out of Chapel Spring Middle School, but above the whole town itself.

The only way to escape the Dog Log was to escape Chapel Spring completely. But how? How does a girl with a crappy bike and no money leave town and start a new life?

I imagined all kinds of crazy scenarios—hitchhiking on a desolate highway, walking through the forest and camping under tree canopies, riding in the back of a bumpy truck while the breeze of freedom blew through my hair—until the answer became clear to me.

When George Harrison was thirteen, his dad bought him a Dutch Egmond flat top acoustic guitar. When he was fifteen, he joined his first band. And when he was sixteen, he left school to make music. Lots of people in history have left their lives behind to follow their dreams. It's been done a million times. Louis Armstrong joined a quartet in New Orleans when he was eleven and became one of the most famous jazz musicians of all time.

And he's not the only one. When I was in elementary school, I went to New Orleans with my mother, and I remember walking through the French Quarter and seeing musicians with their hats and cases full of dollars and coins. I asked my mom why they were playing music on the street instead of on a stage.

"They're making a living," she said. "That's what happens when you don't make good grades. You have to stand on the sidewalk and play music for money."

But the musicians looked happy to me. They tapped their feet and sang their songs and smiled the whole time. When people dropped money in their guitar cases, they said thank you and kept right on singing. They looked like they were having fun. The people listening did too.

So that's what I would do. I would go on the field trip to New Orleans. I would wait for the perfect moment, the perfect opportunity, when no one was paying attention, and I would slip away. Take off. Run. I would run and run and run until my legs couldn't carry me anymore. I would have a guitar on my back, and as soon as everyone stopped looking for me I would find a spot on the sidewalk with all the other street performers, and I would play and play and play until my guitar case was full of money. I could play until my fingertips hurt, and then I could join a band. By that time it wouldn't matter that I'd run off, because people would be tired of wondering about Apple Yengko. And I wouldn't be Apple Yengko anymore anyway. I would be someone else. Maybe I would call myself Ana.

There was one big difference between me and

George Harrison, though. I didn't have a dad to buy me a guitar. And my mom certainly wouldn't show up with an Egmond flat top.

I needed a guitar.

I needed a plan.

7. Because

2FS4N: "Because"

By the time I emerged from my room, Lita was at the house. Lita is a nurse and was able to bring me and my mom to the States because of some kind of nursing-shortage crisis. Lita has been here a lot longer than us though. Twenty years, something like that. She has two daughters. One of them is a senior at the private Catholic high school. She's a cheerleader, makes straight As, serves on the student council, and plays volleyball. She's the kind of girl who makes you think you are totally messing up the whole growing-up thing. Lita's other daughter is in college studying to become a paralegal, so now any time Mom had a legal question, she asked Lita.

Mom and Lita were sitting at the dining room table playing gin rummy when I came in looking for something to eat. When they're together, they speak only Cebuano, and even though I understand a lot of it, I've forgotten a lot too. When we first moved here, my mother said we needed to speak English all the time so we could blend in with the Americans, but pretty soon she started mixing her English with Cebuano. I stuck with English. So much for blending in though. It doesn't matter what language you speak when you're the only Filipino in your school, you're named after a fruit, and you're one of the ugliest girls in school.

The kitchen smelled like garlic, lime, and onions from the fried rice my mom cooked earlier. She uses a special Asian citrus seasoning on her fried rice instead of soy sauce, and it smells like limes. She calls it her "rice secret." She says soy sauce has too much salt. For some reason she is always worried about how much salt we eat.

"Hello," Lita said, without looking up from her cards. Lita was a lot like my mom personality-wise, but they looked nothing alike. Lita was very plump and round, and she always wore the same shade of red lipstick, no matter what.

"Hello, *Manang* Lita," I mumbled. I just wanted to get something to eat and disappear into my room, where I could fall asleep and dream of my reinvented life. But it's never that easy when adults are in the way.

"How was school today, *Analyn*?" Lita asked. I could tell by the tone of her voice—and the fact that she called me Analyn—that they'd just finished talking about me. I could feel the aftermath of their conversation hanging in the air.

"Fine." I took the leftover rice out of the

refrigerator and pulled a bowl from the cabinet.

"Don't take too much, *Analyn*," my mom said. "I don't want to see any go in the trash."

Lita shifted some of her cards. "Anything new happening, *Analyn*?"

Even though they were saying Analyn like it was a joke, I wasn't going to complain about it. Let them say it however they wanted; hearing Analyn was a lot better than hearing Apple. At least *Analyn* Yengko wasn't third on the Dog Log.

"No," I said, filling my bowl with big, heaping spoonfuls.

Now that I was in the room, my mother started speaking English, which meant one of two things: What she was saying couldn't be translated into Cebuano, or she wanted me to hear her clearly.

"At her age I had so many friends, I couldn't go anywhere without them nipping at my feet," she said.

Definitely the wanting-me-to-hear-her thing.

"I know what you mean," Lita said. "At that age friends are very important."

I put my bowl of fried rice into the microwave.

"Apple—eh, *Analyn*," said my mother, speaking more loudly. "Did you know Lita's daughter Olivia had her first sleepover at six years old? Lita's house was always full of Olivia's friends."

"Fantastic," I said, pushing the numbers to set the time.

I've only had one friend over for a sleepover, back when I was eight.

Her name was Iris.

Back then I didn't know any better. I figured all moms mixed vinegar and tuna together and ate it out of the can with a spoon. All moms, I assumed, monitored the water in the bathtub to make sure you didn't waste any. But thanks to Iris, I know better now.

"You and your mom talk funny," she'd whispered to me that night as we sat together eating rice at the dinner table. "Especially your mom. How can you understand anything she says? And what's with this rice?" I remember how she'd wrinkled her nose. "What's in it?"

I'd shuffled the rice around on my plate. "Garlic."

"I've never seen rice look like this," Iris replied. "Where's the gravy?"

I'd walked up to my mother, who was putting two drops of dish-washing liquid into the water in the sink. Like everything else, she monitored how much dish-washing liquid she used.

"Mom, can Iris have gravy?" I'd asked.

"Gravy? What do you mean, gravy?" asked my mother, almost too loudly.

I'd looked back to make sure Iris wasn't listening, but she was still pushing the rice around with her fork.

"There's no gravy. It's garlic rice."

"I know, but can we eat something else?"

"But you love garlic rice."

"Can we order a pizza instead?"

My mother set plates in the drying rack and sighed.

"*Ay naku.* There's food right in front of you."

Iris had other questions too. Why don't you have a dad? How did he die? What kind of language does your mom speak? How did you get to America? Why is your skin so dark?

On Monday Iris told everyone at school that my house smelled like fish and my mom didn't know how to speak English. Every time I passed Iris at recess, she pinched her nose. Pretty soon the other kids did too.

The next Friday my mom asked me if I wanted to invite Iris over again.

"We can order pizza this time," she'd said.

I'd locked myself in my room.

"Apple hasn't had a friend over in a long time," Mom said now, to Lita. "Last one was—whatshername, Apple?—Alexie, I think. That was a long time ago. She comes one time for dinner, and I never see her again."

"*Ay Dios ko,*" Lita said, which means something like ohmygod, youcantbeserious. "Why, Apple? Why aren't you inviting friends for sleepovers?"

Because no one can understand my mother when she talks. Because she eats sardines out of the can with her fingers, cooks Spam in a skillet, and freaks out if someone leaves too much food on her plate or uses too much water in the bathtub. Because she wears an apron that says: *Mabuhay Philippines!*

Because, because, because.

The microwave had five seconds left, but I stopped it anyway and quickly took out the bowl, even though it was almost too warm to hold.

As I left the kitchen Lita said, *"Tst-tst-tst,"* to my mother.

This means: What a shame.

8. The Price of Twenty Dollars

2FS4N: "Money (That's What I Want)"

Right before you steal something, you feel it everywhere. Your mouth gets dry. Your insides rattle. You even feel it in your fingertips. Each one of them tingles.

That's exactly what happened to me right before I took the twenty dollars from Mr. Z's wallet. It happened as soon as I started thinking about it, actually. Alyssa and Gretchen were in the band room with about fifteen other kids trying out for the swing choir. I wanted to watch, but Mr. Z said I would have to wait in his office if I wasn't auditioning.

His office was in the corner of the large band room, which had short bleachers for chorus practice, circles of chairs for the band, and big empty spaces in between so all the music groups of Chapel Spring Middle could be in there at the same time if needed. Because Mr. Z's room was so small and tucked away, it felt removed from everything, and I did too. Especially when I saw his wallet. He'd left it on his desk with the edge of a twenty-dollar bill sticking out of it. It was the exact amount I needed, and there it was. Almost like fate.

I used to count the number of times my mother refused to get me a guitar. Last time I counted, it was up to twenty-two. Twenty-two times. I can't remember the first time I asked, but from then until now, it's been no twenty-two times. You'd think that after twenty-two times, she would know how serious I am.

But she doesn't care. She doesn't understand music. I don't get how someone who doesn't even have a favorite song could have been married to someone who loved *Abbey Road* so much that he wrote his name on the tape in marker and kept it his whole life. She didn't understand. She wasn't like me or my dad, or even Mr. Z. He understood music. That's one of the reasons he was everyone's favorite teacher at school—because he knew what was important. It's not just about math or science or English. Sometimes it's about other things too.

When I finally leaned over and grabbed the twenty bucks, my heart was beating so loudly that I almost couldn't hear Elora Sullivan singing "Oklahoma" on the other side of the door.

It was hard to pull out the money without opening the wallet, but I was too nervous to pick it up, and I didn't want to leave any fingerprints, so I tugged and tugged until it came free, then quickly stuck the bill into the pocket of my jeans and sat down.

I'd never stolen anything before. I'd never done anything at all before, really. I made good grades, and I'd never been sent to the principal's office or been yelled at by a teacher. Not even once. Stealing definitely wasn't something I wanted to do, but how could I ignore fate?

My leg bounced up and down. My heart was going a hundred beats a minute. When I heard Mr. Z call another name, I took my eyes off the office door and looked around his office. A few worn-out instrument cases were shoved in the corner. The books on his shelf were about bands and music. Most of the spines were cracked.

That's when I saw it. I couldn't believe I hadn't noticed it before: a poster of the Beatles' album cover for *Help!* I wondered if that was Mr. Z's favorite album. I wondered who his favorite Beatle was. Probably Paul. Grown-ups always seemed to like Paul best.

I pulled the twenty bucks out of my pocket and

turned it over and over in my hand. Even if it was fate, maybe I'd find another way. Mr. Z could probably use all the twenty-dollar bills he could get.

This time, when I leaned over the desk, I picked up the wallet and opened it so I could put the money back where it belonged. My heart wasn't beating fast anymore, and my fingertips weren't tingling—at least not until Mr. Z opened the door.

"Apple?" he said. He looked at me, his wallet, and the twenty dollars like it was all a puzzle he couldn't figure out.

I opened my mouth to explain, but what could I say? I was holding the wallet in one hand and the money in the other.

"What are you doing?" he asked.

"Uh . . ."

"You'd better come with me," he said. He put the wallet in his back pocket, then led me out of the office, right in the middle of swing-choir auditions. Marie McCarron was standing in front of the group, waiting to audition, but when she saw Mr. Z leading me by the elbow, she stopped fidgeting, and everyone—including Alyssa and Gretchen—watched us leave.

I prayed to become a blackbird and fly away, but instead I made it all the way to Principal Earnshaw's office and waited while he and Mr. Z spoke in another room. Principal Earnshaw walked back in alone and looked at me through his round glasses. His face was scrunched-up so much that I thought they would pop off his nose.

I didn't know what to say or do, so I looked at my Chucks.

"I'm going to have to call your mother," he said. He was looking at his computer. "How do you pronounce her name?" He picked up the phone and dialed.

"Glo."

He studied the screen closely and raised an eyebrow. "Glo?"

"Her name is Amihan, but everyone calls her Glo."

He kept his eyes on the screen and tapped his finger against the desk. My mom didn't answer right away. She was probably getting ready for work.

"May I speak to Glo Yengko, please?" said Principal Earnshaw. He glanced at me like he still didn't believe that was her name. "This is Principal Earnshaw at Chapel Spring Middle School. I have your daughter here and—" Pause. He repeated, "Earnshaw. From your daughter's school?" He nodded. "Yes, I'm the principal. I have your daughter here. . . . Yes, Apple . . ."

He was on a different kind of merry-go-round. The kind where you have to explain things three times, because my mother's English isn't always the best, especially when she doesn't know the person.

"She's in my office," he continued. "If possible, I need you to come here as soon as you can."

She arrived ten minutes later, wearing her scrubs. When she came into Principal Earnshaw's office, she sat in the chair next to me and put her arms around her purse. She always holds on to her purse like someone will snatch it at any minute.

Principal Earnshaw cleared his throat and looked at my mother over the rims of his glasses.

"Mrs. Yengko," he began, "I'm afraid we have a serious matter on our hands."

Out of the corner of my eye, I saw my mom turn her head to look at me, so I focused on the plant against the wall. Two of the leaves were brown.

"Your daughter has been caught stealing," said Principal Earnshaw.

"*Ay naku,*" my mother said. "Stealing what?"

"Money from Mr. Zervanos's wallet."

"*Ay naku!*" She reached over and nudged my elbow so hard that it slipped off the armrest. "Is this true?"

I stared at the plant. The air conditioner came on, and the leaves rustled.

"Who is Mr. Zervanos?" asked my mother.

"The band director," said Principal Earnshaw.

My mother was silent then. All last year I'd begged my mother to let me audition for swing choir. She said no a total of twenty-seven times. Her excuse was always the same—that I needed to focus on homework because "brains get you places, not music." The conversation always began with the same three words: "Education is key."

I once asked why I couldn't go to college and play music at the same time. Maybe I could even get a music scholarship, I'd suggested.

"No time for both," she'd said, and she told the story about how it was snowing when we came to Chapel Spring and how that meant we would have a better life, and to get a better life, you have to have a good education.

"Stealing is a serious offense at this school, Mrs. Yengko," Principal Earnshaw continued. "We may have to consider suspension."

My mother repeated it. "Suspension?"

"Yes. It means she would have to stay home for

three days and would make zeros on all her missed work. It's fairly serious."

When my mother didn't say anything, Principal Earnshaw shuffled the papers around on his desk. "But," he said, clearing his throat, "she is an exceptional student, and she's never been in any trouble, so we'll just suspend her for the rest of today."

My mother glared at me. "Come, *Analyn*. Time to go home for suspension."

"Okay, then," said Principal Earnshaw, because my mother was now standing and tugging on the back of my shirt so I would stand up too. When my mom decides a conversation is over, it's difficult to regain control. The principal tried his best though. He quickly stood. "I will suspend her for the remainder of the day, and this is going into her school file. If anything like this happens again, it will be a five-day suspension."

"Thank you, Mr. Shaw," said my mother.

As soon as we got into the car she launched into

a Giant Mom Lecture. These lectures usually started with the word *oy*, which loosely translates to "I simply can't believe it" in English.

"Oy, Apple," she said, shaking her head. "It's no wonder you have no friends to the house. You change your name for no reason, and now you steal money from teachers. You are a good girl, *anak*. Why did you do this? Children in the Philippines never steal from their teachers. We help sweep the floors and clean the classrooms every morning and every afternoon. That's the problem with America; they don't teach children respect. They spoil them. No hard work. In the Philippines, children have respect for adults . . ."

In my mind I screamed, *This isn't the Philippines!* as loud as I could. I screamed it until my throat was sore and all the windows in the car shattered.

"You can be known as Analyn the Thief or as Apple, a good American girl," said my mother. "Your choice."

I looked at the sky. It was bright blue with a round, perfect sun. I imagined a hole cracking open and transporting me into another dimension so I wouldn't have to listen to my mother. A dimension where I was starting a new life. Maybe, in the other dimension, I would form a four-person band and play lead guitar. Maybe, in the other dimension, there would be no such things as mothers or suspensions. There would be no Dog Logs. There would just be me. And I would be happy.

9. Turning American

2FS4N: "I Will"

The thing I remember most about the Philippines is the water. It's the most beautiful water you'll ever see. It's sparkling shades of green and blue and feels like it covers the whole world. I can remember the way it smelled too—salty and wet—and how the sand felt when it pushed between my toes. Sometimes I wonder what my life would be like if we had stayed there. My mother says she wanted us to have a better life, but when I think of splashing through the water and eating mangoes until the juice dripped down my chin, I don't understand how our life in America is any better. In the Philippines, I would be just another face in the crowd. No one could call me a dog-eater or a dog. Maybe I would even be pretty.

My mother says we came to America because there's more opportunity, but the real reason we came is because my dad died and my mom didn't want to be reminded of him. That's why she said we needed to leave everything behind; she was worried that if she took my father's watch or his beat-up tape player she would just keep remembering how much she missed him. Maybe it's because she wasn't prepared for him to die. It was sudden. A brain aneurysm. For years I was convinced that I would die of a brain aneurysm too.

I would've taken my dad's old tape player, but it was bulky. So I took *Abbey Road* instead and that old postcard.

I used to take out the postcard a lot and imagine that we'd never left the Philippines, but I've put so much stuff in my drawer that I can't even see it anymore. I've learned that it's not good to remember things. You have to look forward. That's what I'm doing. That's why I'm going to New Orleans. I'm going to reinvent myself in a whole new city, surrounded by music and new people. Jake Bevans won't be there and neither will Braden or Lance or any of their idiotic friends. While I'm playing my guitar, everyone in Chapel Spring will be talking about how I ran off and disappeared and was living like an adult, and Alyssa would be so jealous that she wouldn't know what to do with herself. For once the big announcement would be about me.

I pulled my red notebook out of my weekend backpack and stretched across my bed. I was just about to start writing out a new guitar-getting plan when my mother knocked on my door. I don't know why she bothers knocking, because she always comes right in. Every time she does, I get a tight feeling in my chest like I want to scream.

She sat on the corner of the bed. "What's wrong?"

I flipped my notebook shut; it closed with a loud *clap*. My mother looked down at me. It was almost nine o'clock, and we hadn't spoken since the car ride home.

"Nothing," I said.

She sighed and frowned. "Apple, what's going on with you?"

"Nothing."

"Why did you steal that money? The Yengkos aren't thieves."

"How would I know?" I mumbled. "All the Yengkos are in the Philippines. Only we're here." Here in this crappy town, in this crappy house, with my crappy bike and our crappy napkins.

My mother crossed her arms. "Take my word on it then, *Analyn*." She glared at me. "What's the matter with you? You don't have any friends over; you're stealing from teachers; you're changing your name. You are turning into another Apple Yengko. Maybe you are turning American, I don't know."

If she knew anything, she'd know that the problem wasn't that I was turning American, it was that I wasn't American enough. Nothing about me was American except my address and my school, and those things don't even belong to me. Not really.

"What happened to your friends?" she said. "You used to have friends. I remember."

It's because of you! Because you talk funny and you cook weird food and you aren't normal like the other mothers! If I had an American mother, my life would be easy, like Alyssa or Claire or Gretchen! Instead I'm the third-ugliest girl in school!

The reasons turned into a big lump in my throat. I swallowed them away.

"Did you decide to quit speaking too?" she asked.

"No," I mumbled.

She raised her eyebrows and kept glaring at me. Waiting for me to say something, I guess. But nothing would come out. Finally she sighed again and walked toward the door.

Before she closed it, I said, "I tried to put the money back." But she didn't hear me and shut the door behind her.

10. Little White Lies

2FS4N: "Not Guilty"

The next day I walked slower than usual to my locker. I'd ignored Alyssa's phone calls the night before, and even though I hoped she had some kind of grand announcement of her own that would make her and Gretchen forget that I'd been dragged from the band room by Mr. Z, I had a feeling that my departure would be the first topic of discussion.

I was right.

"What *happened*?" Alyssa said, leaning against Heleena's locker as Gretchen riffled through her stuff as usual. "You never came back."

I'd planned to tell Gretchen and Alyssa that I'd come down with some kind of twenty-four-hour virus. But just as I opened my mouth to talk about my mysterious affliction, Alyssa tilted her head suspiciously and told me she'd heard something that "just couldn't be true."

"I heard Mr. Z caught you going through his stuff," she said. "But I was like, what could Mr. Z possibly have that you would even want?"

"I wasn't going through Mr. Z's stuff." I swallowed. "I just didn't feel well. I was about to get sick in his office, so he got me out of there. I thought I might faint."

Alyssa narrowed her eyes. "I heard you were going through his wallet."

I laughed, but the laugh didn't sound like mine. It sounded shaky and unnatural, like someone had planted it in my mouth. I wished I could just tell them the truth—about how my mom had said no to a guitar twenty-two times and I didn't have any money to buy one myself and I felt desperate and wanted to run away and be like George Harrison—but I couldn't. Maybe if I had different friends, I could. But Gretchen and Alyssa don't even like the Beatles. I played *Abbey Road* for them once, and they didn't even make it to "She Came in Through the Bathroom Window." They said the music sounded weird and dumb and they didn't see what the big deal was.

"Why would I go through Mr. Z's wallet?" I said.

"I don't know," Alyssa said. She looked at Gretchen. "Didn't you hear that too, Gretchen? That Apple was caught going through his wallet?"

"I'm going by Analyn now," I corrected, but they ignored me.

"I don't know," said Gretchen. "If Apple says she was sick, then she must have been sick."

Alyssa bit her bottom lip and glared at me, still

suspicious. "You would tell me if you were in trouble, right?" she said. "We're friends, remember?" She lifted her pinkie finger the way she used to when we first became friends. Before all she cared about was being popular. It didn't look right now, her holding up her pinkie like that. It used to, but it didn't now.

I linked pinkies anyway. "Yeah, we're friends."

"If you're in trouble, you have to tell us," she said. "We're best friends." She and Gretchen linked pinkies too. "The three of us."

I nodded. "I know."

"You definitely don't need any more notoriety right now," said Alyssa, bumping hips with me. "Right?"

"Right."

"I'm still working on getting all that cleared up, by the way. No way you're a number three. And this is the worst thing that could possibly happen right before the dance. You can't go by yourself when me and Gretchen have dates, can you? That would just be the most embarrassing thing ever."

"She can if she wants to," Gretchen said. "Maybe we should just all go as a group. That might be more fun. Don't you think, Apple?"

Alyssa shook her head and said, "I'm not going with a group. Jake asked me to the dance and I'm going with him on a real date, not as some group thing like a bunch of fifth graders." She rolled her eyes as if Gretchen's idea was the dumbest thing ever, then turned to me. "You better pray you get a date to that dance, Apple. It might be your only hope of redemption."

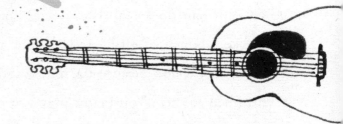

11. Redemption

2FS4N: "From Me to You"

When the lunch bell rang, I made a beeline for the library so I could look up *redemption* on the computer. I usually asked Gretchen to Google on her smartphone when I needed information, but I didn't want her to know that I didn't know what the word meant. I'd spent my morning classes thinking about what Alyssa had said, and even though I wanted to forget all about the stupid

Dog Log and go on with my life, I couldn't. Alyssa was right.

redemption (n): the action of being saved from sin or error; something that saves someone from error

I wasn't sure if the error was me, the Dog Log, or both, but I definitely needed saving.

I stared at the screen and the word *redemption*. I heard someone mumble hello. I looked up.

It was Evan, the new kid.

"Hey," I said.

He did a quick wrist-flick wave before heading straight for the books.

I looked back at the computer. *Redemption.*

Question: Who would take an ugly girl to a dance?

Answer: A boy who didn't know any better.

I found Evan standing in one of the aisles with his head tilted to the side. He was reading book spines. I cleared my throat and sucked in my belly to stop it from flipping. Part of me wanted to cry, part of me was nervous, and part of me thought Evan was really cute. All these parts mixed together to create a big jumble of nausea in the pit of my stomach.

"Hey, Evan," I said, smiling broadly. Fake smiles always feel weird, like someone is pulling up the corners of my mouth with fishing wire. "Did you finish *Silmarillion*?"

"No, but I'm ready for something else," he said. "Not sure what, though."

"Oh."

I considered turning around and bolting, but I couldn't move. He stared at me like he was waiting for me to explain myself. When I didn't say anything, he went back to reading the book spines.

"My name is Analyn, by the way."

He didn't look away from the books. "I know. You told me, remember? A-N-A-L-Y-N."

"Oh yeah." Could I be a bigger dork?

"But I thought I heard your friend call you something else. Apple, I think?"

"Yeah, that used to be my nickname." I rubbed my finger along some of the spines, just to have something to do.

"What do you mean 'used to be'? Usually when someone has a nickname, they have it for life."

"I decided to drop it. Start going by my real name—Analyn."

That was the third time I'd told him my name. I was getting more ridiculous by the second.

"Why?" he asked.

"Just because. It was time for a change."

He shrugged. "Apple's pretty cool. I never heard that nickname before. How'd you get it?"

I picked at the loose binding on a book called *The Blue Girl*. I wondered if it was a book about a blue-skinned girl, a depressed girl, or a girl with the last name Blue.

"It's an embarrassing story," I said. I pulled *The*

Blue Girl from the shelf; as soon as I did, Evan leaned over to see what I'd selected. I put it back in a hurry.

"It's better than Evan Temple," he said. "At least your name doesn't sound like a place people go for church."

I laughed. My laugh sounded nervous and weird, like I was having an out-of-body experience.

"It's because I have a big head," I explained. "Round, like an apple. That's what my mom says anyway."

He looked at my head and blew his hair away from his face. "It doesn't look big to me. It looks like it weighs between seven and nine pounds, which is average. I'd estimate that if we put your head on a scale, it'd come in around three-point-six kilograms."

"Oh," I said.

He took a step closer, pulled *The Blue Girl* from the shelf, and started to read the dust jacket.

"Is the girl blue, or is she depressed?" I asked.

"Skin's blue," he said. He tucked the book under his arm. "Are you Filipino?"

For a second I wasn't sure I'd heard him right. All my life people have asked me where I'm from, what ethnicity I am, if I am Chinese or Latina, but this was the first time someone actually knew.

"Uh, yeah," I said. "How'd you know?"

"Because you look Filipino. How else?"

"It's just . . . people around here don't usually know what I am."

"There's tons of Filipinos where I'm from. One of my best friends from back home is Filipino. His name's Raoul Gonzales, but everyone calls him Bon-Bon. He moved to the States when he was in the fourth grade. What about you? Were you born in the Philippines? You don't have an accent."

"I was born there, but we left when I was little."

"Cool."

He tried to head back to the desk to check out his book with Mrs. Fastaband, the librarian, but he didn't get too far, because I was in his way.

"I'm going to check out my book now," he said, waiting for me to move out of his path. I didn't move though, because I needed to put my plan into action.

My mouth opened, but no words came out.

"Um." He raised his eyebrows.

"Er . . . uh," I said.

"Are you okay?"

No, I thought. *I'm the biggest dork in America. No, the world. I'm the biggest dork in the world.*

"Yeah. Sorry. I kinda blanked out." I stepped out of his way.

"That's okay," he said, walking past me with the book under his arm. "See you around, Analyn-Apple."

"Er . . . uh," I said.

I peeked around the bookcase and watched him give *The Blue Girl* to Mrs. Fastaband. She punched some buttons on the computer while he tapped his foot and blew his hair out of his eyes. When he spotted me, I turned away as fast as possible. I wondered if I would have a heart attack right there in the Chapel Spring Middle School Library. Would Mrs. Fastaband leap up from her desk and save me?

"Apple?"

I turned. Evan was standing there.

"Yeah?" I said. My throat was dry. I swallowed, but it didn't help.

"Are you sure you're okay? You're acting weird. Then again, maybe this is how you act all the time. I wouldn't really know."

"Well . . . actually . . ." My body felt hot from the inside out. What if I started sweating? What if a puddle formed around my feet? What if my face turned so red that he thought I was choking? What if it was red now? It was hard to tell what I looked like from the expression on his face.

"Actually what?" he asked.

Time to just blurt it out and get it over with.

"You wanna go with me to the Halloween dance?"

"I thought the boys were supposed to ask the girls," he said.

I shrugged. "I guess so, but . . . well, I don't know . . ."

I was definitely the biggest dork in the world. No, the universe.

"Do I have to wear a costume?" he asked.

"Yes. Well, no, not if you don't want to. . . . I mean, I was gonna wear one, but you know, whatever."

"Okay then," he said.

We looked at each other silently.

"Maybe you should give me your number." He took his phone out of his pocket. "You know, in case we need to get in touch and stuff?" He opened the screen for a new contact. His hair fell around his face. Without looking up, he said, "Okay, what is it?"

I couldn't remember my number. Was it four-oh-five-five or five-oh-four-four? Or maybe it only had one four and one five. But wasn't there a three somewhere? Oh god. I had to say something.

"Uh," I said. I considered shouting out random numbers, just anything, so I wouldn't keep standing there like a moron, but even random numbers wouldn't jump into my head. My entire brain was empty. All except, "Uh. Um."

He looked up. "It's hard to remember your own number sometimes, since you never call yourself."

I chuckled. Another out-of-body experience. "Yeah."

And then they came to me: all the fours and fives and threes in the right places.

At least I *think* they were the right places.

After he put my number in his phone and we said our awkward good-byes, I waited until he left the library before I walked out too. My heart didn't stop pounding until I was back to my normal life, which meant sitting with Alyssa and Gretchen under the oak tree in the quad.

"Where were you?" asked Alyssa. "We looked all over."

She took a swig of her Diet Coke. Usually she drank Dr Pepper, but as soon as the school had announced the Halloween dance, she switched to Diet Coke. She said she had to watch her weight.

"We were just discussing the spring swing-choir show," she said. "I decided to stay in, because Mr. Z says we're doing *Grease* this year and I'm up for Sandy."

"Oh. Great." Hearing Mr. Z's name made my cheeks warm.

"If I get it, I just hope that Jake doesn't get too jealous about me singing with another boy. He can be *so* overprotective when he likes someone."

I glanced around the quad to see what Jake was up to. He was standing against the north wall, knocking Jane Domino's braids off her shoulders while she slapped his hand away. He didn't seem too interested in anything Alyssa was doing.

"I have a date to the dance," I said.

Gretchen's eyes lit up. Alyssa glared at me—suspicious but full of curiosity.

"Who?" Alyssa asked.

"I don't really want to go with him, but he just asked me in the library, and I didn't want to hurt his feelings." The fib spilled out without warning. Little white lies, but with each word that came out of my mouth, I felt more and more like Analyn the Thief.

"Who? Who?" Alyssa said.

"Yeah," Gretchen said. "Who?" She scanned the quad as if she could guess who my date was simply by looking around.

"Evan Temple," I whispered.

"Ohmygod!" said Alyssa. "I can't believe you're going with him."

"I couldn't say no," I said. "He looked like he really wanted to go." It was amazing how easily the lies came out now, like I'd been lying my whole life.

Gretchen nodded knowingly. She knew all about breaking boys' hearts.

"Of course you couldn't say no," Alyssa said. "He's your only hope."

"What are you going to dress up as, Apple?" asked Gretchen.

"I don't know."

"Gawd, can you imagine what Evan might be?" said Alyssa. "He'll probably be all decked out in some kind of devilish freak costume. How embarrassing."

"It doesn't matter," I said. "I don't like him or anything."

"Good. Because Braden isn't going with anyone, and he kinda asked if you had a date."

My heart dropped. "Braden? Really?"

Part of me was elated. Even though I was on the log, Braden had asked about me and he was one of the most popular guys in school.

Then again, he was also one of the most idiotic.

But still.

"Yeah," Alyssa said. "Jake told me that Braden asked if you had a date to the dance. I said no. So I asked Jake if Braden wanted to ask you, and Jake said Braden didn't want to go with anyone in particular, but he was planning to ask you to dance with him on a couple slow songs."

I bit my bottom lip, thinking about all this new information. Ever since Braden had nicknamed Mr. Ted "Sweaty Teddy," and especially since the day of Alyssa's party, I'd thought Braden was a jerk, but suddenly he transformed into something different. Alyssa was with Jake. Gretchen was with Lance. It would be amazing to have a boyfriend in the same crowd—the *right* crowd. Dating one of the popular guys in school was sure to get me off that stupid Dog Log. And maybe Braden wasn't all that bad.

"Maybe you could ditch Evan once you get to the dance. You know, nothing too harsh, but just like sneak away and dance with Braden real quick," said Alyssa, taking another sip of her Diet Coke.

"That doesn't seem like a nice thing to do," said Gretchen.

"Evan is a jerk anyway." Alyssa tossed her hair

off her shoulder. "Remember?"

"Maybe he won't mind if I dance with Braden," I said. "I mean, it's not like I'm married to Evan. I just need him. For redemption, ya know?" Even as I said it, it didn't feel like me saying it. I don't know who it was. I felt like I was someone different, someone I didn't like that much but someone who was still trying to be better all at the same time. If you lie and still have good intentions, it's still almost okay—right?

12. Cleopatra

2FS4N: "Maxwell's Silver Hammer"

A few years ago, my mother spent an entire afternoon watching a really long movie about Cleopatra. My mom never took her eyes off the TV except during the commercials, when she would go to the bathroom or load the dishwasher or grab a quick snack of sardines from the pantry, all in a big rush so she could get back to the movie. Personally I thought the show was super boring. All except

Cleopatra. She was so pretty, I could hardly believe it. Dark, dark hair and eyes like crystals. She didn't look like the other actresses in the other old movies my mom liked to watch, but she was prettier than all of them put together. At least I thought so. That's why I decided to be Cleopatra for Halloween.

My mom had an old dress that she said I could wear. All it needed was a few pins here and there to make it fit right. And I had something I could use as the headdress. It was a beaded headband that Alyssa had left in my bag after one of her dance recitals at the beginning of sixth grade. She said she didn't need it back, so I just tossed it in my closet and forgot about it. When I got the idea to use it for Cleopatra, I went through an entire greatest-hits anthology digging around in my closet to find it.

After that the main thing was the eyes. Cleopatra wore dark eye makeup and eyeliner that made her eyes look wide and enchanting. I pulled up a picture of Cleopatra on the computer and set it next to my dresser mirror so I could get it just right. I'd never had so much makeup on my face in my entire life, but I didn't mind. I felt like I was covering up all the things that made me ugly.

When I was done, I stepped in front of my mother's full-length mirror and couldn't believe it. I looked like myself but not. Maybe I wasn't as gorgeous as Cleopatra, but I didn't feel like a girl on the Dog Log either. I imagined Alyssa's and Gretchen's faces when I walked in. Even the boys would be amazed. Maybe.

The only thing is, I didn't have any Cleopatra-like shoes, so I wore my Chucks. The dress was just long enough to cover them.

I wondered what Evan's costume would be. I half expected Gandalf or Bilbo Baggins. Instead here's what I saw when I opened the door: a white T-shirt and blue jeans. A red stripe went straight down the T-shirt, and another red stripe went across it, but the horizontal stripe wasn't just on the shirt. It was also across the insides of his forearms. He was wearing his Vans. A woman stood behind him with her hands on his shoulders and a smile so wide that it looked like she had a thousand teeth. Her hair was the same color as Evan's, and her nose was shaped the same way. *It must be nice,* I thought, *to know where all your traits come from.*

"Wow," he said, looking my costume up and down. "Cleopatra?"

"Yeah. What are you?"

He raised his arms. The red stripes made a T. "I'm a plus sign." He jutted a thumb over his shoulder. "This is my mom. Her name's Anna."

Anna exploded in hellos as she and Evan stepped into our living room. His mom smelled like the art room at school. Nothing like the smell of Filipino food that had buried itself into the walls of our house. I tensed and looked at Evan, waiting for a reaction, something that might tell me he planned to pinch his nose for the rest of the school year. But he just looked around like it was normal. I was suddenly aware of everything in our house: the weird Santo Niño in the cabinet, my mom's map of the Philippines on the wall, the dull-looking furniture in the living room, our small kitchen table with its one slightly wobbly leg. My house felt completely different with Evan here, like I was sharing a secret I wasn't ready to tell.

"I'm so glad Evan is going to the school dance with you, Apple," his mom said. She put an arm around me. The bangles on her wrist jangled. She had on a long dress covered in flowers and splattered with paint. "You look gorgeous! Just like Elizabeth Taylor."

My mom smiled wildly as they made the usual introductions.

"I couldn't believe it when Evan told me he was going to a school dance already," said Anna. She had the happiest smile I'd ever seen. "I was worried it would take him a long time to adjust, but he seems to be doing okay, going to the dance with a pretty girl and all." She glanced down at her dress. "As for me, I look a mess. My apologies. I can't help it much though. All my clothes are a nightmare."

"You should use our dry cleaner. They're very good and won't rip you off," said my mother.

She started telling Evan's mother all about our dry cleaner. Of all the things to talk about. My embarrassment grew to epic proportions. I didn't want to look at my mom, Evan, or my house, so I focused on one of the flowers on Mrs. Temple's dress instead. It was a daisy that looked like it was being eaten by a big glob of white paint.

"I'm an artist, so it's no use trying to keep anything clean," said Anna. "I paint."

"Oh, a painter!" said my mother. "What do you paint?"

"Abstracts, mostly."

"That's a fancy word for paintings that don't make any sense," Evan mumbled.

His mother shot him a scolding glance.

Evan and I sat at the almost-wobbly table next to each other as our mothers exchanged numbers and started talking about stuff like Evan's dad and his new job. Evan chewed on his fingernail. I ran my hand over my hair. I had to put extra conditioner in it to make it softer before I straightened it. It felt weird.

"How come you told your mom my name was Apple?" I whispered to Evan.

"Sorry, I guess I forgot," he said, still chewing. "But it's just because you look more like an Apple."

Was he saying I had a big head? I didn't ask.

"It's neat that your mom's a painter," I said. "I bet she's good at it."

"If you like crazy paintings that don't look like anything," he said, brushing his hair away from his forehead. I wondered why he didn't just cut his hair if it bothered him so much. "Sorry about her clothes. She's always covered in paint or has chopsticks coming out of her head. She's kinda weird."

I thought about her big smile, how she smelled

like the art room, and all the bright paint stains. I wondered what it was like to have a mom who loved to create things. I bet she wouldn't have any problem with Evan learning how to play an instrument, even if it was something out of the ordinary, like the organ or the harp. I bet she had a favorite song.

"She seems really cool," I said.

"I guess," Evan replied.

Mrs. Temple offered to bring us to the dance, and I prayed that she would, but my mom insisted on driving us there.

"I love driving around," said my mother. "In the Philippines, I didn't have a car. I walked everywhere— down to the store, down to the river, down to my friends' houses—because everything was close together. Then I came to America and learned how to drive. I learned quick." She snapped her fingers. "And now I love it. I even cheat the speed limit sometimes. Right, Apple?"

I wanted to die. I jumped up from the table so quickly that it rattled. I was ready to get to the dance and show off my Cleopatra costume, but mostly I was ready to get out of the house and away from my mother.

Finally Evan's mom left, and we got in the car. Evan stared out the window while my mom quietly hummed. As if she wasn't embarrassing enough.

She dropped us off in front of the gym, which was decorated with spider webs and guarded by Principal Earnshaw, who was dressed as a pirate.

"Be sure to say hello to the principal so he can forget about what happened," said my mother as Evan and I got out of the car. She waved like a maniac to the pirate, who didn't see her.

Evan and I walked down the sidewalk leading to the gym entrance. I heard music thumping from inside the building.

"Why does your mom want you to say hello to Earnshaw?" Evan asked.

"It's a long story," I said.

I made a point not to say a word to the principal when we passed him by.

13. Dedications

2FS4N: "Sgt. Pepper's Lonely Hearts Club Band"

The gym had been transformed. Multicolored strobe lights bounced red, blue, and green across the room. Loud music blared from every corner. Refreshment tables lined the wall, and crowds of people danced, laughed, and stood around. The only thing that looked the same was the gym floor. Even though it was dark, you could still see the free-throw lines for basketball. And the bleachers still stretched from the floor to the ceiling. A few kids sat on them, but most everyone was in the middle of the dance floor.

Another thing that was the same was the smell. It still smelled like sneakers and basketballs.

Evan and I walked in slowly, mostly because I was taking my time. My plan had been to break away from him somehow by disappearing into the crowd, but that seemed stupid now. Maybe I didn't have to ditch him. Maybe he could just hang out with us and it would be okay.

I ran my hand over my hair.

"I like your mom," said Evan. The loudspeakers were right by the door, so he had to shout over the music. "It must be cool to have a mother from another country. Sometimes I think my mom's from another planet, but it's not really the same thing."

"She can be a little embarrassing," I said.

"Yeah, I know, but what can I do? I tell her to not go out in public looking like that."

I smiled. "I was talking about my mom, not yours."

"Oh," Evan said. He laughed.

"Sometimes people have trouble understanding my mom because of her accent. It can be kinda embarrassing," I said.

"Maybe they're just not listening hard enough."

Before I could reply, we were spotted by Alyssa, Jake, Gretchen, Lance, and Braden. Alyssa was Dorothy from *The Wizard of Oz*. Gretchen was dressed as a zombie bride, and the boys were all ninjas. Alyssa waved us over, and the whole group eyed us as we walked up. I turned to the side casually so they could get a really good look at my Elizabeth Taylor eyes.

"Hey," Alyssa said flatly.

Jake pointed at Evan. "Who're you, and what are you supposed to be?"

Evan raised his arms. "Evan Temple, plus sign."

Everyone snickered. Alyssa looked at me over her glass of punch.

"Is that my old headband?" she asked.

I touched my headdress. It had been perfect for the costume, or so I thought. But now Alyssa looked at it like it was stolen, even though back in sixth grade she'd told me I could keep it.

"Your costume's great, Apple," said Gretchen. "You look just like an Egyptian princess or a Greek goddess."

"She's Cleopatra," said Evan.

Jake and Lance snickered again.

"Cleopatra?" said Jake. "I thought she was a Chinese restaurant owner or something."

Gretchen glared at him.

"Apple's Filipino," said Evan.

"So?" Braden said.

Evan shrugged. "I'm just saying, she's not Chinese, she's Filipino." He looked at Braden, who threw back his shoulders and narrowed his eyes. Braden was a foot taller, but Evan barely blinked. The bouncing and flickering lights made Braden look like some kind of middle-school boogeyman, dressed all in black. He liked to pick fights. It was one of his IFs.

I hoped someone would say something to change the subject. I wanted that someone to be me, but for some reason nothing was coming out of my mouth. Instead I watched Danica Landry, Elora Sullivan, and Marie McCarron walk toward the snack table. Danica was dressed as a genie, and Elora and Marie were both cats. They looked at my costume but didn't say anything about it as they passed by.

"I heard they're doing dedications starting at nine o'clock," said Gretchen.

Braden relaxed his shoulders and stepped away from Evan. "Oh, yeah?" he said. "What kind of dedications?"

Alyssa glanced at Jake when she answered. "You get on the mike and dedicate a song to someone, and they'll play it. How sweet would that be, to have your date dedicate a song to you? If some guy did that for me, I'd never forget it."

Only, Jake wasn't listening, because at that moment Heleena Moffett entered the gym. She was dressed like a woman from the 1800s, with a big, round skirt and ringlets in her hair. My heart dropped the way it does when you know something bad is about to happen. The dress was light blue, and the hoop skirt made her look even bigger than she already was.

She walked slowly, like she didn't know where to go.

"Ohmygod," said Jake. "Look at this. It's Big-leena."

Everyone turned in Heleena's direction.

Alyssa's face lit up like Christmas lights. "Ohmygod," she echoed. "And she's totally alone. Why even come?"

"Of course she's alone. Who would want to show up with an extra planet of the solar system?" said Lance.

"Well, she's number one, right?" said Braden. "How much do I get for slow-dancing with that?" he mumbled to Jake.

"That's double the money, easy," said Jake, snickering.

No one but me was paying attention to Jake and Braden—they were too busy watching Heleena heave herself around the gym and plop down on the bleachers.

I turned to look at Heleena too. *Please get out of their sight, Heleena. Braden is going to ask you to dance all because of a dare. If he asks, please say no. He's only doing it because you're number one on some stupid list.*

Wait a minute.

I snapped my gaze away from Heleena and looked at Alyssa. She was still making some joke about Heleena's dress, but her words were all garbled.

How much do I get for slow-dancing with that?

I remembered lunch, stupid lunch, when Alyssa told me that Braden kinda asked Jake about me.

Double the money, easy.

Braden never wanted to dance with me. He was getting something for dancing with girls on the Dog

Log. It was a dare. I was a joke. Something to laugh about.

My eye makeup suddenly weighed a ton. The headband felt like a bull's-eye. I was aware of every pin in my dress, ready to stab me. If only I hadn't come. If only I could fly away. Fly, blackbird, fly.

Jake let out a loud and deep bark in Heleena's direction.

"Dog incoming!" he hollered.

"Yeah," called Lance. "Who let the dogs out?"

Lance cupped his hands around his mouth and barked as loud as he could. I wrapped my arms around my stomach. I felt sick.

Evan leaned closer to me as the others hooted and hollered. Thankfully Heleena was too far away, and their voices were drowned out by the booming music.

"Are you okay?" Evan asked. "You have a weird expression on your face, like you're about to throw up."

Maybe I was wrong. Maybe that's not why Braden asked about me. Maybe he really wanted to dance with me. Maybe I wasn't some stupid dare. Maybe.

"Hey, Big-leena!" Jake called out as loud as he possibly could.

"Who's Big-leena? And what's the big deal with her?" Evan asked me.

"Heleena Moffett," I said, even though that wasn't really an answer.

Evan glanced over at the bleachers. I could tell by his expression when he spotted her. His face didn't light up like Christmas lights. Instead he frowned and glared at the others.

"I dare you to dedicate a song to Big-leena," Jake said to Braden.

Lance nodded. "Yeah! Do 'Who Let the Dogs Out.'"

"They would never play that," said Braden.

"Something else then," said Jake. "I dare you. When dedications come up at nine."

Heleena looked at her feet as everyone moved past her. It was just like in the hallways at school, except here she was a lonely Southern belle surrounded by superheroes, witches, ninjas, and cats. I wondered what she was thinking about. I'd had gym with her last year, and it seemed like she hated it more than any place on earth. She always walked onto the basketball court like it was powered with electrodes.

"She looks like the fattest blueberry I've ever seen," said Alyssa. "My mom could bake a hundred pies with a blueberry that big."

"More like a thousand," said Jake.

I leaned toward Gretchen. "You can't let them dedicate a song to Heleena," I whispered.

Alyssa heard me. "What do you mean *we* can't let them?" she asked.

"Tell them not to."

Gretchen glanced toward Lance and bit her bottom lip, which was decorated with jagged blue lines that were supposed to look like veins.

"If it's so important to you, Apple, then *you* tell them," said Alyssa.

"They won't care what I say. You need to tell them how stupid it is."

When Alyssa didn't respond, I looked to Gretchen. "Gretchen, can't you talk to Lance? He can tell them how stupid it is."

"What's stupid is this conversation and the fact that you're still here with Evan," said Alyssa. "Especially when Braden wants to dance with you."

"He doesn't want to dance with me. It's just some bet he made with your idiotic boyfriend to dance with girls on the Dog Log."

Alyssa put her hands on her hips. "Idiotic?"

"Yes. Idiotic."

"Who cares? You should just be happy someone wants to dance with you."

I felt like I'd been slapped in the face. I didn't know what to say. Neither did Gretchen. She stared at me with big, pitiful eyes. The music switched tempo, and I heard a laugh from far away. It was a happy laugh, like someone had just told a hilarious joke, not a mean one. I wished I was standing next to that person, whoever it was.

"What happened to you?" I said to Alyssa. "You used to be . . . different."

"I grew up," she said. "This is the real world, Apple." Her Dorothy pigtails bounced as she turned on her heel and went to stand with Jake.

Gretchen whispered, "I'll ask Lance not to."

But something told me she wouldn't.

Evan was standing there by himself, and I stood next to him. I knew we were both thinking the same thing: They couldn't play that joke on Heleena. They just couldn't. So even though they might not listen to me, even though I was ready to wash off my face, run home, and cry on my bed, even though my two so-called best friends wouldn't like it, I had to say *something*.

But I didn't get a chance.

"She actually thinks she looks *good*. That's the funny thing," said Alyssa.

Evan crossed his arms. "She looks better than you."

Alyssa looked at me, like he was my responsibility. "Excuse me?" she said.

"She looks better than you," said Evan again.

Jake stepped in front of Alyssa and crossed his arms too. "What is that supposed to mean?" he said.

"I'd dance with Heleena before I'd ever dance with some evil, second-rate Dorothy."

Alyssa's mouth dropped open. So did Gretchen's.

"As if I would ever dance with you anyway, freakboy," said Alyssa. She turned back to me with eyes as thin as razors. "I thought you said you were gonna ditch this freak and dance with Braden."

Braden whipped his head around in surprise. "What?" he said. "Who said I wanted to dance with—" He and Jake exchanged looks and laughed—a laugh that bordered on a howl and bounced off the gym floor and banged against every wall. I heard the laugh and nothing else, not even the music.

"*You're* the freaks," said Evan.

"Why don't you just get outta here anyway, surfer boy?"

Braden pushed Evan—hard. There was a screeching sound as Evan went sailing across the gym floor on his butt and the heels of his hands. When he came to a stop, his arms were extended and he looked very much like a plus sign.

We all stared at him—not just me, Gretchen, and Alyssa, but a whole bunch of other kids. The music thump-thumped along as Evan looked up at everyone from the gym floor, and I knew I had a decision to make: I could help him or I could stand there with everyone else.

Evan pushed himself up with his left hand.

I walked over and grabbed his right.

"California boy's got a guard dog!" hollered Jake.

Braden threw his shoulders back and barked. His

barking was louder than the slow song that was just starting up. Lance took Gretchen's hand. Jake took Alyssa's. Braden stopped barking and wandered off, still laughing. I hoped he wasn't looking for Heleena.

Evan and I stood there next to each other as the lights dimmed. We probably looked like we were about to dance too, if someone didn't know better.

"What did she mean?" Evan asked, brushing off his pants.

"Who?"

"Evil Dorothy." He wiped gym grime off his palms and frowned at me. "About ditching me for that blockhead."

"I don't know," I said.

"Why would you ask me to a dance if you wanted to go with someone else?"

This was the time to say something that would make me look like a decent human being, but I couldn't come up with anything, because I felt just like the dirt that Evan had brushed off his hands.

"Your friends suck," he said. He blew at his hair and sighed. "It's really crappy to ask someone to a dance and then ditch them. Do you think I *want* to be at this stupid thing?"

"Why did you come then?"

"Because you asked me, and I thought you were interesting. Guess I was wrong," he said.

When he walked away from me, he didn't sulk or hunch over or make a big deal of it—he just walked off. I watched him disappear across the gym. Then I headed to the girls' bathroom on the other side of the building.

The hallway was dark and smelled like textbooks and metal lockers. It was strange being there when it was empty and all the lights were out. It felt wrong, somehow, but there was really nowhere else for me to go—I couldn't rejoin Gretchen and Alyssa, Evan was gone, and I had no other friends.

I went into the girls' room and sat on the counter, even though I knew I was probably ruining my mother's old dress. Who cared? They were right. I was no Cleopatra.

I thought about New Orleans. I imagined strumming a guitar and singing until my voice blended in with all the sounds of the city. No one would know me there. Maybe I could meet other musicians and join a band.

I tried not to cry, I really did. I had all that eye makeup on. I'd listened to "The Fool on the Hill" five times on repeat when I put the makeup on, because that's how long it took. Now I really was the fool. But not on a hill. Sitting alone on a bathroom countertop with my Chucks dangling out of a stupid Cleopatra dress held together with pins to make it look just right.

I cried anyway. My makeup would smear, but so be it. I thought about calling my mom to pick me up early, but then she'd know something was wrong, and that was the last thing I needed.

I wished I had a marker. A big, fat, black marker.

If I did, I'd march into one of the stalls and write something terrible about myself. I deserved it.

I was thinking about all the terrible things I would write when the door opened. This bathroom was really out of the way, so it was the last thing I expected. Heleena came in, bringing the distant sounds of music with her. She was looking at her feet, so she didn't see me until the door closed and she looked up. Then she stopped.

I sniffled and wiped my face in a big hurry. Not like it mattered. My Cleopatra makeup was everywhere. I could tell.

"Hey," I said.

"Hey," said Heleena.

I scooted over as she walked up to the row of mirrors behind me. She narrowed her eyes at all those ringlets and started pulling out her bobby pins, one by one. The ringlets fell flat against her round face.

I studied my shoes and felt my nose run. I couldn't hear the music from the gym anymore. All I heard was the sound of her dropping the bobby pins in the sink. *Plink. Plink. Plink.* Then she took off her shoes. I could tell that they were brand-new.

She stood there, barefoot. Then she reached into the belt of her antebellum gown, pulled out a handkerchief, and handed it to me.

"You can keep it," she said, picking up her shoes.

And she walked out the door, leaving all the bobby pins behind her.

14. Sayings

2FS4N: "Yesterday"

I didn't hear from Alyssa or Gretchen for the rest of the weekend, but to be honest, I didn't really care. I spent most of the time in the safety of my room, where I thought about all sorts of things: ugly-girl lists, the Philippines, Jake and Braden and Alyssa, what I'd done to Evan, what I'd done to Mr. Z, running away from everyone on the field trip. Everything.

I listened to *Abbey Road* and put "Here Comes the Sun" on repeat. I listened to "Yesterday" and "Because" and dreamed of leaving.

I thought about my dad too. I wondered if he had listened to music when bad things happened to him. I wondered what his favorite Beatles song or his favorite all-time song had been, and what he would have said about boys like Jake, Lance, and Braden.

I thought about Heleena and her bobby pins.

My mother didn't bother me until Sunday night.

"Apple?" she said, knocking lightly on the door.

The fact that she knocked on the door and didn't open it told me she knew something was wrong. But I would never tell her about the Dog Log. I would rather shrivel up and die.

"Is everything okay? I've hardly seen you since the dance."

I turned up my music. "I'm fine."

A pause. Then she opened the door, but just a crack. I quickly wiped my hands over my cheeks.

"There is a saying in the Philippines," she said. "Maybe you remember it. It says, 'It's never too late to offer something good.'"

"We're in America. People don't eat dogs here, and they have their own sayings."

She shut the door without saying anything else.

I stared at the ceiling.

It's never too late to offer something good.

But what did I have to offer? Music that I didn't even know how to play?

I reached over to my laptop. I'd only planned to switch the playlist, but instead I went online to see what the rest of the world had to say about how to play guitar.

15. Where Friendless People Go

2FS4N: "While My Guitar Gently Weeps"

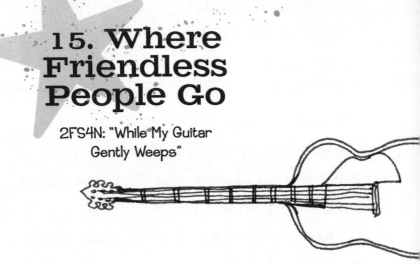

Gretchen's locker is at the farthest end of the south hall, so every morning since the first day of school, Alyssa and I have stopped at our own lockers before meeting up at Gretchen's. On the Monday after the school dance, I closed my locker, slipped my backpack over my shoulder, and made my way down the hall as usual. I wasn't sure what to expect, but I wasn't all that surprised when they both immediately

turned their backs on me. They huddled in front of
Gretchen's locker shoulder to shoulder and acted like
they were discussing something really important. As I
passed by I heard Alyssa whisper and giggle.

I kept walking.

In homeroom Braden was the same doofus he
usually was. It was like the dance hadn't happened.
That's how it always is for the people on the other
side.

When the lunch bell rang, I made sure to take
the long way to my locker so I wouldn't have to pass
Gretchen's locker again. I passed Evan a couple times,
but he just walked by like I wasn't there.

I wished I wasn't. I wished I was on my way to
my new life instead of going to the library for lunch.
According to Alyssa, that's where the "losers" go
when they have no one to sit with.

Heleena was there, sitting in a corner, wearing
earbuds and reading. I wondered what she was
listening to.

The only other person there was Mrs. Fastaband, who was sitting behind her desk. When she saw me, she asked if she could help me find anything. I thought about asking if she knew of any good holes I could crawl into. Instead I asked if the library had a music section.

"Looking for anything in particular?" she asked.

"Something about guitars, maybe. Like the different kinds and how to play them."

I expected her to say no, because our library isn't very big, but to my surprise she pointed to a section next to the biographies. There were two books on how to play guitar. I pulled both of them from the shelf and was walking toward a table when Evan entered the library and headed to the biography aisle. When he saw me, there wasn't much he could do. It's hard to do a freeze-out one-on-one.

"Hey," he mumbled, and kept walking.

"Hey," I said, to his back. There was a tight knot in my stomach, and my palms got sweaty as I watched him turn the corner. *I'm sorry, Evan. I don't know why I did the things I did.*

I sat silently at a table and opened *Teach Yourself Guitar.*

I'd found plenty of videos online that gave lessons on how to play guitar, but it was tricky to learn anything when you don't have an actual instrument. The book was tricky too. I tapped on the pages with my pencil and stared blankly at the diagrams. It was hard to concentrate anyway, knowing that Evan was just a few feet away. I knew I should go apologize, but I couldn't bring myself to get out of the chair.

I pulled my red notebook out of my backpack. I usually kept it in my weekend backpack, but every now and then I brought it to school for emergencies. I figured today would be an emergency, and considering that no one except teachers had spoken to me all day, I was right.

On the first blank page, I wrote *Guitar-Getting Plan* at the top, but after several minutes of staring at the carved graffiti on the library desk (*school sux*, it said), I had only two ideas: Strike up some kind of bargain with my mom or save up my lunch money until I had enough to buy one.

Lunch ticked by slowly. Time moves differently when you don't have friends. I thought about Gretchen and Alyssa under the oak tree, Alyssa eating her Funyuns and Gretchen sticking her empty Skittles bag in her pocket. When a lump formed in my throat, I swallowed it away and pushed the heels of my hands against my eyes so I wouldn't cry. That's all I needed—to start crying right there in the library with Evan in the aisle nearby.

When there were ten minutes left of the lunch hour, I walked over to Heleena. She didn't seem surprised to see me. She just took out her earbuds and looked up. Kind of smiling, kind of not.

"I know it's annoying when people interrupt when you're trying to listen to music," I said, motioning toward her earbuds. "But I just wanted to say thank you for letting me borrow your handkerchief. I'd give it back, but it's got makeup all over it. Maybe I can buy you a new one."

"It's okay," she said. "It cost only a dollar."

"Your costume was really cool. I meant to tell you that."

She smiled. "I liked yours too."

"Except for the runny nose and smudgy eye makeup."

"Yeah." She laughed. It was probably the quietest laugh I'd ever heard. "Except for that."

When I left Heleena's table, there were still seven minutes left of lunch. I checked out *Teach Yourself Guitar* from Mrs. Fastaband. Instead of going back to my locker, I turned left.

To the band room.

Since I wasn't allowed to be in swing choir, take music lessons, or do anything except "real subjects," as my mom called them, I didn't spend too much time in the band room, but I thought it was the best room in Chapel Spring Middle School. It smelled like old instruments, probably because there were dozens of them everywhere—saxophones, trumpets, flutes, clarinets, trombones. There was an old drum set in the corner, even though no one ever played the drums for band, and a piano on the other side of the room. Sheet music was scattered around, some pages with only a few simple notes and others with hundreds—so many that I wondered how anyone could ever play it. There were also instrument cases of all shapes and sizes and different kinds of oils, cleaners, and reeds too.

When I got there just before the end of lunch bell, the room was empty.

I'd written an apology to Mr. Z the night before. I figured I would leave the note under his door and get out of there as soon as possible, considering what had happened to me the last time I was in the band room, but I got distracted by a French horn. It was hanging on the wall, all rusty and beat-up. I stopped to examine the keys and study how the pipes twisted and turned all the way up to the spout, or whatever it was called. I didn't touch it though. With my luck the whole thing would have come crashing down.

If not for that French horn, I would have been in and out of the band room in a flash, but instead I was still there when Gretchen and Alyssa walked in for swing choir.

"Hey, *Cleopatra*," said Alyssa, with a snort. "What are you doing here?"

I slipped the note for Mr. Z deep in my pocket and held the thick guitar book close to my chest.

"Nothing. Just came to talk to Mr. Z about something."

"Are you sure you just wanted to 'talk'? Or maybe you're running short on cash and you wanted to pop in and see if Mr. Z left his wallet out again?" She crossed her arms. Gretchen stood next to her, looking straight at me without saying a word. "I saw you put something in your pocket."

I looked at the clock on the wall.

"I'm not a thief," I said.

"That's not what I heard." Alyssa rolled her eyes. "You're practically a juvenile delinquent. It's a good thing me and Gretchen aren't hanging out with you anymore. We have reputations, you know." She nodded toward my pocket. "So what did you steal, *Apple*? Did you find a tiny guitar that would fit in your pocket for you to take home?"

"I didn't steal anything," I said. A sick, warm feeling moved up my body to my neck and cheeks.

Alyssa nudged Gretchen with her elbow. "Maybe it's a love letter for freakboy. Maybe this is where they meet. Their secret love hideaway."

"Shut up," I said.

Alyssa stuck out her hand, palm up. "Hand over whatever you stole, or I'm gonna turn you in to Mr. Z."

"I didn't steal anything."

"Hand it over, or I'll tell the whole school the truth about you being a kleptomaniac."

The guitar book slipped out of my arms and slammed onto the floor. The loud *thump* made all of us jump, but even worse it made Alyssa squeal in a weird, surprised way, which made Gretchen giggle.

"Give me what's in your pocket, klepto!" Alyssa yelled, coming at me.

We both fell. I'd never been in a fight before— never even close—so I had no idea what to do. The first thing I did was cover my face with my arms, which was when Alyssa went into my pocket and pulled out the note. When she stood up, I was still on the ground.

Alyssa unfolded the note. Gretchen read over her shoulder.

I found my footing and stood up. "Give me that!"

I snatched it from Alyssa just as the bell rang. Marie McCarron came in humming. She stopped when she saw us. Others came in behind her, along with Mr. Z. They all looked confused to see me there, since I didn't belong.

"What's going on in here?" Mr. Z asked, looking at my red, angry face and at Alyssa and Gretchen standing in front of me. He took long strides toward us.

"Nothing, Mr. Z," said Alyssa. "We came in for rehearsal and we caught Apple in here going through all the band things. Right, Gretchen?"

Mr. Z looked at Gretchen. She didn't say anything.

He turned to me. "What's going on here, Apple?"

"Nothing, Mr. Z. I just came to—"

"—to steal something," said Alyssa. "She has a serious problem, Mr. Z."

"That's enough, Alyssa. Why don't you find your place?" He waved his hand toward the bleachers, where most of the members of the swing choir now stood, watching us curiously.

"Did you need something, Apple?" asked Mr. Z quietly.

I handed him the note—crumpled and ripped in one corner—and ran out, holding back tears.

I heard Alyssa yell, "Ugly thief!" just before the door closed behind me.

It wasn't until later that night, when I was eating dinner, that I remembered I'd left the guitar book on the floor of the band room. What a perfect way to end a perfectly terrible day.

"You not feeling well?" my mother asked as I threw my leftover dinner noodles into the trash. Usually she scolded me if I threw anything away, but this time she didn't. She just watched me over her magazine.

"I feel fine," I said. I put my bowl in the sink and hoped to escape to my room without answering any more questions.

"How was school today?"

"Fine."

"How is your friend? The boy."

"Fine."

"Is that all you can say? 'Fine'?"

"No. I can say other things. Like Fender Starcaster. But you don't want to hear that, so I just say 'fine' instead."

"Apple." She put down her magazine. "What are you talking about?"

She would know what a Fender Starcaster was if she would ever listen, but she never did, so I went to my room, turned on some music, and took out my notebook. It was time for another apology note. This time, to Evan.

The first draft took up almost a page—it explained how sorry I was and why I asked him to the dance— but it rambled on and sounded like nothing but a load of excuses, so I crossed it out and started again. The second note was shorter but more apologetic. I mentioned how much my mom liked him and how cool and interesting I thought his mom was. I even started explaining my IF theory. But that note didn't feel right either, so I crossed it out too.

I tapped the end of my pencil on the paper, then

turned my music even louder than usual. I don't know why. Maybe because I was angry and sad all at once. I turned it up and up and went back to my paper and wrote just two words: *I'm sorry.* I signed it *Analyn, aka Apple.*

Then I turned off the light and, even though it was only eight o'clock, I crawled into bed. I closed my eyes and imagined myself relaxing on a white sand beach. I heard Alyssa's voice calling out *thief,* and I imagined the word rolling off with the waves, into the deep blue sea.

16. Sorrys

2FS4N: "Being for the Benefit of Mr. Kite!"

The three most interesting IFs I could come up with about most of my teachers are pretty boring. Ms. Bonnabel, for example, loves to say, "Believe you me." Like, "If you don't quiet down, there will be trouble, believe you me." I have no idea what it means, but during one class I kept count of how many times she said "believe you me," and I swear she said it ten times. At least.

Miss Lattis eats bananas before class. Mr. Teche makes clicking sounds with his tongue when he's thinking. Mrs. Henry is super clumsy—she drops her dry-erase marker at least three times per period, and she usually runs into the bookcase next to her desk at least once.

Besides Mr. Ted, who is interesting in his own weird way, the teachers at my school have an uninteresting list of IFs. But there is at least one cool teacher at every school in America. This is the teacher that all students want for history, science, whatever. The teacher laughs *with* them instead of *at* them. At Chapel Spring Middle School, it's Mr. Z.

For some reason apologizing to a teacher I liked seemed harder than apologizing to one I didn't. As I walked up to the band room after fourth period I wished I was apologizing to Ms. Bonnabel or Mr. Teche.

It was a big day for apologies. I had already slipped my note to Evan into his locker, and now I opened the door to the band room slowly and peeked inside.

The last thing I needed was to barge into a crowded room, blurting out my "I'm sorrys." Mr. Z was in his office. I could see him through the open door.

My heart thumped with every step.

"Mr. Z?" I said. My voice was small.

He looked up and tossed some papers on his desk. Sheet music.

"Yes?"

I played with the straps of my backpack.

"Did you come for your book?" he asked.

"Uh . . ."

"I have it right here." He turned around without getting up from his chair, slid *Teach Yourself Guitar* off his shelf, and placed it on the desk in front of me. I picked it up and hugged it to my chest.

"Thank you," I said.

He leaned back in his chair. "Is that all, Apple?"

"No," I said. "I also wanted to say again that I'm sorry about the twenty dollars. It was wrong for me to take it. I tried to put it back. That's what

I was doing when you walked in."

"Hm," he said. "Why were you so desperate for twenty dollars anyway?"

I clutched the book. "I don't know."

He sighed. "So you tried to put it back?"

I nodded.

"Okay," he said. "Fair enough."

I turned around to go.

"Just one more thing, Apple . . ."

In the span of two seconds, a million thoughts went through my head: *Just one more thing, Apple—you should be imprisoned for life. Just one more thing, Apple— you are a menace to society. Just one more thing, Apple— never set foot in my band room again. Just one more thing, Apple—what kind of stupid name is Apple anyway?*

". . . if you've never played guitar before, it might be easier to learn from a teacher instead of a book. Everyone learns differently, but that's how I did it."

I let out a deep breath and turned back around to face him.

"If you bring in your guitar, I can give you some lessons during lunchtime or after school," he said.

"Uh . . ."

"Any day but Tuesdays, because I have another student on Tuesdays. How's that sound?"

Fantastic. There's just one problem. I don't have a guitar.

"Great," I said. "Thanks, Mr. Z."

"No problem, Apple."

I didn't even care that he called me Apple. All I cared about was taking him up on his offer. Somehow.

17. Goddess of the Dog Pound

2FS4N: "Penny Lane"

We go to school eight hours a day with only an hour of freedom—otherwise known as lunch. I wasn't in love with the idea of spending my forty-five minutes in the library again, so I decided to go into the quad and figure out my next move. I needed to show everyone that I wasn't afraid. I couldn't spend the rest of my life with Fastaband, after all.

Unfortunately Jake and Lance were walking to the quad at the same time.

"Hey, goddess of the dog pound," said Jake as they passed by.

Lance laughed and smacked him on the back.

I turned around and headed to the library.

Mrs. Fastaband smiled when I walked in. I wondered if it made her happy to see students come to the library during their free time. There weren't many kids at Chapel Spring Middle School who wanted to hang out there, that's for sure.

I sat down and pulled out my notebook. The library can be a lonely place when you're by yourself, and I was really by myself. Heleena wasn't even there.

I guess any place is lonely when you don't have any friends.

Luckily I had a lot to think about. My first order of business was to revisit my Guitar-Getting Plan, which didn't take long, since there were only two things written down. I stared at my notebook for a while, waiting for a fantastic idea to magically appear. When it didn't, I doodled a few guitars for inspiration. I even drew a Dutch Egmond flat top. I also drew a Fender Starcaster acoustic, which is the one I really want one day.

"Cool guitars," said Evan.

I stopped midsketch. I hadn't even noticed him walk in. Suddenly I was embarrassed by my doodles, even though Evan's head was tilted toward my paper and it seemed like he really did think they were cool.

"How come you're not outside with Evil Dorothy?" he asked.

"We're not really friends anymore."

"They didn't seem like they were your friends in the first place."

"I guess not."

"I got your note," Evan said. "Since you're in the library, I guess that means you're friendless now, huh?"

"Yeah, I guess."

He sat across from me. "Not anymore." He ran

his fingers through his hair and stacked his books on the table.

It's amazing how quickly an accepted apology can change a relationship.

"Why're you drawing guitars?" he asked. "Do you play guitar or just draw them?"

"I want to be a songwriter like George Harrison."

"Who's George Harrison?"

"George Harrison was one of the Beatles." I raised my eyebrows. "You've heard of the Beatles, right?"

"Of course. My dad listens to them sometimes, I think. They have a weird song about a yellow boat or something." He shrugged.

"'Yellow Submarine.'"

"And there's that other song too, the one about a girl named Penny."

"'Penny Lane.' Except it's not about a girl. It's about a street by John Lennon's house. John Lennon was another one of the Beatles. He's my second-favorite."

"He's the one who wore those little glasses, right?"

"Right."

"So why is George Harrison your favorite? I've never even heard of him."

"That's because he was more in the background. But that's why he was the best. He wrote all these great songs, but he didn't make a big deal about it. He wrote one of my favorite Beatles songs of all time— 'Here Comes the Sun.' 'Blackbird' is my number-one favorite, even though it's not written by George Harrison, but 'Here Comes the Sun' is almost just as good. One day I'm gonna learn how to play both of them on the guitar."

"My mom tried to get me to take music lessons once. She also tried to get me to paint. But I'd never want to do what my mom does. She has all these paintings of shapes that are all different colors. Big deal. It's stupid, if you ask me." He leaned way back in his chair and chewed on his fingernail. "I'll show you what I *really* want to do."

He opened his backpack, reached deep inside, and pulled out a model airplane. He set it on the table between us.

I leaned forward and looked at it. It could have fit in my hand, but I didn't want to risk touching it. It was completely painted. Even little details.

"I want to build things like airplanes and trains and stuff. Real airplanes, not little ones like that," Evan said.

"Wow," I said. Through the tiny, little windows I saw tiny, little seats and there were even tiny, little instruments in the cockpit. "You built this?"

"Yeah."

He returned it to his backpack.

"I've been building a lot more of them since there's not much to do around here," he said.

"I bet you miss your friends in California."

He nodded. "Especially Bon-Bon. He taught me how to say five different curse words in Filipino. Do you know any?"

I smiled. "No."

"I'll teach you one." He cleared his throat, then blurted out: *"Atsara!"* He said it with gusto, like he was really angry and cursing. He beat his fists in the air and said it again, *"Atsara! Atsara!"*

"What's it mean?"

He shrugged. "I have no idea."

By the time lunch was over, I knew at least one of Evan's IFs: He wasn't afraid of anything. Not that I could tell, at least. When I asked if he'd been scared of Braden at the dance, he looked surprised, like it never occurred to him.

"No," he said. "Why would I be? He might be bigger than me, but he's dumb."

"He might be dumb, but he could have knocked you out."

Evan shrugged. "Let's say he broke my nose. Big deal. My nose will recover, but he'll still be dumb."

"Weren't you embarrassed?"

"No."

"If someone had pushed me down in front of the entire school, it would have been the most embarrassing moment of my life."

"You shouldn't care so much what people think," he said.

"I don't."

"Yes, you do."

"Okay, maybe a little bit. But everyone cares what people think."

"You're right. Everyone cares. But if you waste too much time worrying about Evil Dorothy and her zombie bride, your brain cells may never recover."

The bell rang, and we gathered our books. We walked out of the library in silence, but just before we split up in the hall, I said, "Did you really think my mom was cool?"

"Yeah," he said. "Don't you?"

I shrugged. "If you ever want to come over again, she said it was okay."

"Okay," he said. "Well, see you later, three-point-six."

"Three-point-six?"

"Yeah. It's the size of your head, remember? In kilograms. Normal size. I'm still calling you Apple though."

I didn't argue.

18. Stew

2FS4N: "Don't Let Me Down"

After spending two nights flipping through *Teach Yourself Guitar*, I decided to implement Guitar-Getting Plan A: Strike up a bargain with my mom. I had a feeling it wouldn't go my way, because it never had before, but you never know. Sometimes parents surprise you. Well, moms do. I wouldn't know about dads.

After a night reading about chords that I couldn't

practice and watching online tutorials that I couldn't imitate, I carried my book into the kitchen, where my mother and Lita were playing cards at the dinner table.

The kitchen smelled like fried egg rolls. There was a plate of them in the middle of the table. The paper towels were wet with grease.

"Hello, Apple," said Lita, without looking up from her cards. "I hear you went to a school dance with a nice boy." She smiled. "I remember my first dance." She swayed in her chair like she'd gone back in time. "What about you, Glo?"

My mom shrugged. "Only the dances that mattered most," she said. A strange look came over her face. It was the remembering look.

"I hear the boy is nice *and* smart," Lita said to me.

My mother's face cleared. "Better to have a smart man than a handsome one," she said.

Lita nodded. "Yes, yes. Handsome boys are much more trouble." She shuffled her remaining hand. "Is he your boyfriend then, Apple?"

"Her name is Analyn now, remember?" said my mother, glancing at me.

"Oh, yes. I keep forgetting."

"No, he's not my boyfriend," I said. "Just a friend."

"Olivia had her first boyfriend when she was your age." Lita tapped the corner of her eye. "I kept my eye on them, though."

I watched them play a few hands, wondering how best to put my plan into action. My mother seemed like she was in an okay mood. Now was as good a time as any.

"Hey, Mom?"

She glared down intently at her cards. *"Mmm?"*

"I was wondering if there was anything you needed done around the house. You know, like chores you keep putting off or whatever. Something that I can help with."

Lita raised her eyebrows. "Maybe your daughter isn't so American, after all, Glo!" she said, laughing.

"Mmm," said my mother.

"You wouldn't even have to pay me in cash or anything," I said.

My mother concentrated on her cards. "Why would I pay for something you should do anyway?" she said, without looking up. "All children should do chores."

Lita nodded approvingly.

"What I mean is, if you maybe get me that guitar, I could do some extra work. Anything around the house. Even if it's scrubbing the floor. It's only twenty dollars."

"Not after what happened," my mother said. She shook her head and clucked her tongue, as if to say *shame-shame*.

"I apologized to Mr. Z. He not only accepted my apology, he offered to give me lessons. *For free.*" I figured that would get her, but her expression didn't change. "If you get me a guitar, you don't have to get me anything else ever. That's the only thing I want."

"No," said my mother.

"Why not?" I asked.

"Because I say."

"But I can't be a songwriter if I don't have a guitar." *And I can't run away without one either. I'll never get out of Chapel Spring. This will be my life forever. But this can't be it. It just can't.*

"Music is a waste of time, *Analyn.* How many times do I have to tell you? Tell her, Lita. Tell her she needs to spend more time on books and less time worrying about guitars. I came here so she could have a better life—go to college, make money."

I put my book on the table. It landed with a loud thud. "This is a book about guitars, Mom. See? I've been studying for days."

My mother played a card. She didn't look at the book. "You're a smart girl. No need for things like this. They don't get you anywhere. They don't get you money. They get you stuck."

"I'm already stuck."

"That's enough now. Get your elbows off the

table and put the egg rolls in the refrigerator." My mom likes to end conversations with a chore and criticism.

"You don't understand anything," I said. "All I want is a guitar." I looked at Lita. "I've been studying this book. I can have lessons for free. She won't even listen."

Lita glanced at the book and shrugged like, *What can I do?*

I went back to my room without putting the egg rolls in the refrigerator.

There's a saying in the Philippines that my mom used to tell me when I was in elementary school and she wanted to make sure I made honor roll: "If you persevere, you'll have stew."

In other words: If you don't give up, you'll get what you want.

In other words: I was getting a guitar whether she liked it or not.

19. The Apple Yengko Fender Starcaster Donation Fund

2FS4N: "The Long and Winding Road"

After I found out about the Dog Log, I was convinced that people were staring at me, but when I went back to school the following week, I definitely felt like people were giving me strange looks. It started right after third period. I walked out of science class as usual and got a weird vibe, like everyone was talking about me behind my back.

Evan met me at my locker. I told him about it, in case he'd heard something.

"What do you mean, a vibe?" he asked.

"Don't you ever get a weird feeling that people are talking about you? Like, you can't really figure it out, but something seems off?" I put my science book away and took out English and math.

Maybe people were still talking about the Dog Log, but that didn't seem like the answer.

"Yeah, sure. But that's because people usually *are* talking about me. They're like, 'Who's that handsome lad in our midst?' And then I'm all—"

"I'm serious, Evan. It's really bugging me."

Two kids who played trumpet in the band walked by and glared at me. When they were out of sight, I nudged Evan's arm.

"Did you see that?" I said.

He looked around. "See what?"

"Nick Preston and Colby Matthews just looked at me funny."

"I'm sure it's your imagination," said Evan.

It wasn't.

During English, the PA system buzzed, and the secretary asked me to report to the office. As soon as she said "Analyn Yengko," everyone turned and looked at me. My heart plummeted. I hadn't done anything wrong. I'd been on my best behavior since the incident with the twenty dollars. But when you get called to the office unexpectedly after weird hallway vibes, it can't be good.

When I got to the office, the secretary told me that Principal Earnshaw wanted to see me. Another really bad sign.

It got worse.

Gretchen and Alyssa were sitting next to each other across from Principal Earnshaw's desk. I sat in an empty chair next to them. Mrs. Hill, the school counselor, was in the office too, but she was standing with her arms crossed. She smiled at me, but it wasn't a cheery, hello smile. It was more like an uh-oh-I-wouldn't-want-to-be-you smile.

Principal Earnshaw leaned forward. His chair creaked.

"Analyn," he said. "Gretchen here has misplaced her purse, and I was wondering if you knew anything about it. She says the last time she saw it was in the gym."

I looked at Gretchen. When my eyes met hers, she turned away.

"I haven't seen it," I said. "I don't go to gym until after lunch, but I can look for it when I get there."

Alyssa snickered.

"Alyssa said she saw you near the gym after second period," said Principal Earnshaw.

"I got some chips from the vending machine. But I didn't go inside."

Alyssa stomped her foot. "She took it! I know she took it!"

My mouth dropped. Me—steal Gretchen's purse? I looked at Alyssa, Gretchen, Mrs. Hill, and Principal

Earnshaw, one after the other, in a panic.

"What are you talking about?" I asked. "Why would I do that?"

Alyssa narrowed her eyes. "Maybe you were looking for more lip gloss."

Mrs. Hill put up her hand. "I think you should step outside, Alyssa. This really only concerns Gretchen, since it is her purse."

"Yes, yes, good idea," mumbled Principal Earnshaw.

Alyssa made a noise that almost sounded like a huff but wasn't completely a huff. I'm sure she knew that if she made too big of a stink, she'd get in trouble. As she walked out with Mrs. Hill she glared down at me and whispered, "Kleptomaniac."

"I don't understand." I looked at Gretchen. "Do you think I took your purse?"

"If you promise me you didn't take it, I'll believe you," she said.

"Why would I take your purse?" I asked.

Gretchen looked at her feet. "Alyssa said she saw you by the gym, and it looked like you were carrying something under your arm. She said she called your name, and you ran off real fast, like you were trying to get away."

Principal Earnshaw raised his eyebrows at me.

My cheeks were hot, and my insides quivered.

"That's not true!" I said. "And why would I take your purse anyway?"

"You took that twenty dollars from Mr. Z," whispered Gretchen.

"That's different," I said. "I was trying to put it back."

"I'll just ask you simply, Analyn," said Principal Earnshaw. "Did you take Gretchen's purse?"

"No."

"If we find out differently, you'll be suspended for five days. Do you understand?"

"Yes, sir."

Principal Earnshaw turned to Gretchen. "I think

we should take Analyn's word on this until it's proven otherwise. Meanwhile, I want you to make a list of everything that was in your purse when it was taken." He pushed a pencil and a sheet of blank paper across the desk.

"I didn't take it, Principal Earnshaw," I said. "I swear."

He nodded. He looked like he believed me, but I couldn't be sure. My body was on fire. I'd never been so angry. As if I would take Gretchen's stupid purse! She forgot it somewhere at least once a week. Anybody could have taken it. She didn't even have anything to steal, unless you were a thief who liked to wear peach lip gloss and berry-and-roses blush.

"It's possible the purse will turn up," said Principal Earnshaw as Gretchen scribbled on the paper. "In the meantime, we'll just consider the matter unresolved." He nodded toward the door. "You can go back to class."

When I walked out, Alyssa was sitting in one of

the chairs outside his office with her legs and arms crossed. When she saw me, she narrowed her eyes.

"I know you took it," she said.

"Why are you out to get me all of a sudden? I never did anything to you, except be your friend," I said. "You're the one who—"

"The one who what? Got on the Dog Log and went to a dance with some weirdo? That's not me, *Apple*. That's you." She turned away.

I didn't leave immediately. I stood there for a few seconds and looked at her even though she wasn't looking at me. When she had first moved here, I was her only friend. We used to share pinkie promises and stuff our faces with popcorn. We sat cross-legged on the carpet of her house and ate peanut butter out of the jar with oversized spoons. We jumped on the trampoline and giggled for hours.

I thought I hadn't done anything to her, but I was wrong. I *had* done something, even though I wasn't really the one who did it. I got myself on the Dog

Log, and that meant she was tainted because she was my friend. She wanted to move up the tiers, and I was one of the things she was getting rid of so she could. Just like she got rid of the T-shirts and busted-up sneakers she used to wear when I first met her.

I thought about her party. I thought about all kinds of things. I thought about Evan and what he'd said and done at the dance.

He was right. He was *so* right.

"You suck, Alyssa," I said.

I walked away before she could answer, but something told me she wouldn't have anyway.

Evan scrunched up his nose. "You look horrible."

I put my backpack on top of the library table and sat across from him. We had an unspoken lunch routine now: no meal, just the library. Occasionally we brought snacks from home or got something out of the vending machine, but mostly we skipped lunch altogether and spent the time reading books or talking about stuff. I told him about the Beatles, and he told me about hobbits and Middle-earth and airplanes. Meanwhile, I stashed my lunch money, saving up for the guitar. My mother would freak out if she knew I wasn't eating lunch, but then again she's never tasted the lunch at my school.

"Are you okay?" asked Evan.

"Not really." I didn't want to tell him what had happened. Mostly I was afraid that I would start crying. If only three o'clock would come, so I could go home and cry alone. Maybe I'd even try writing a song about it. A lot of great songs are sad songs, like "Yesterday" and "The Long and Winding Road."

"That weird vibe I was getting this morning wasn't my imagination."

I told him the whole story.

"Why would Evil Dorothy call you a kleptomaniac? And why would she accuse you in the first place? No one would ever believe that you'd steal something."

I pressed my lips together.

"Unless there's something you're not telling me," added Evan suspiciously.

"Kinda. But before I tell you this, I want you to know that I am *not* a thief."

I told him everything—about my dream to be a songwriter, almost stealing the twenty dollars, and the one-day suspension. I left out only two details: my idea to run off during the field trip and the fact that I was on the Dog Log. If he knew about that, I'm sure he would find a reason to quit hanging out with me.

He listened to everything as he chewed on his fingernail.

"Wow," he said, when I finally shut up. "I can't believe I went to the dance with a criminal."

I stared at him, and he laughed.

"You don't think I'm a kleptomaniac, do you?" I said.

"Of course not," he replied. "Have you explained all this stuff to Mr. Z? About how you tried to put the money back?"

"Yes. He even offered to give me free guitar lessons."

"So when do you start?"

"I haven't started yet. I don't have a guitar."

"Just borrow one from Mr. Z."

"I'm not going to ask to borrow something from someone I got caught almost-stealing from," I said. "That would be beyond embarrassing."

"So what are you going to do?"

"I'm saving my lunch money. Eventually I'll have enough to buy the guitar."

"Good idea," he said. He reached into his pocket and pulled out a crinkled dollar bill. He pushed it across the table. "For the Apple Yengko Fender Starcaster Donation Fund."

Sometimes trouble comes as no surprise. But sometimes trouble arrives unexpectedly. That's what happened when Evan and I turned down the south hall after lunch. Jake and Lance were standing in front of my locker with their arms crossed.

"Oh, great," Evan muttered.

"Let's just keep walking," I whispered, keeping my head down. "Don't make eye contact."

"But—"

"*Shst.*"

"—you can't let them—"

"*Shst.*"

Evan heaved a big sigh. As we got closer I repeated quietly: "Remember. No. Eye. Contact."

The funny thing is, even when you're not making eye contact with people, you can always tell when they're looking at you. When we walked past, I felt their eyes on my back.

"Hey, dog-eater!" Jake called out.

Evan's head swiveled in Trouble's direction. It took him less than five seconds to disregard the no-eye-contact rule.

"Don't walk away from us, klepto! We wanna have some words with you."

Evan stopped and turned around. Everyone was rushing to class and the hallway was thinning out, but a handful of kids turned in our direction. I thought about bolting, but I couldn't leave Evan standing in the middle of the hall.

"Shut up, you boorish doofus," said Evan.

Silence.

"You and your dog-eating girlfriend better give Gretchen back her purse," said Lance. He and Jake headed toward Evan, their sneakers squeaking against the linoleum.

Evan crossed his arms. A small crowd formed around us.

Jake and Lance stopped on either side of Evan, pushing me out of the way, but Evan didn't budge an inch. He kept his arms crossed and his eyes focused. He looked like some kind of middle-school superhero.

Jake shoved a finger in Evan's chest. "Your dog-eating girlfriend is an ugly thief."

"Sorry, but I don't have a dog-eating girlfriend," Evan said.

"Yeah, you do," Jake said. "Right here." He reached over and yanked a lock of my hair. I immediately jumped back and smacked his hand away.

Jake laughed. "Wow, you got a lotta bite for a puppy." He reached over again, but instead of yanking my hair, he jabbed me under my ribs. *"Yip! Yip! Yip!"*

Evan stepped between us. "It's nice to see that you've expanded your vocabulary beyond the usual grunts, but if you do that again, I'm gonna have to pummel your face. Which might be an improvement, but still."

Jake threw back his head and laughed. "Yeah, right."

"I'm not kidding."

"Looks like you're the guard dog now," said Jake. He reached around Evan and yanked my sleeve. *"Yip! Yip!"*

"Stop it!" I said.

Ms. Bonnabel rushed over, arms waving, and immediately broke up the crowd. "What's happening here? What's happening?" she asked.

"Nothing, Ms. Bonnabel," Lance said. "Just trying to get to class." His face looked angry and red.

She glared at all of us suspiciously. "Okay, get going, get going," she said.

"You can't let them treat you like that," said Evan, when Jake and Lance were out of earshot. "You're letting them get away with too much."

What did Evan know? It was easy for him to say.

"Well, I don't need a boy to protect me," I snapped. "You just don't understand. You're not the school freak."

He snorted. "Yesterday I went to the office to pick up the necessary forms to start a Model Airplane Youth Builders Organization. You think I don't know what it's like to be an outcast?" He shook his head. "There's only one difference between how I deal with boneheads and how you deal with them, and it has nothing to do with me being a guy or you being a girl or both of us being freaks."

"What is it then?" I asked.

"I don't listen to anything they say, because I know that whatever they think about me is wrong," he said. "But you think they're right."

That was the last thing he said before we went our opposite ways to class.

20. Klepto and Freakboy

2FS4N: "I Am the Walrus"

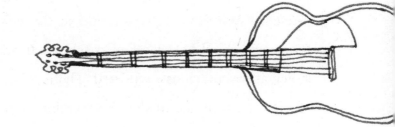

Morning announcements aren't usually all that interesting. These days I used that time to doodle guitars in my notebook.

We always end with the Pledge of Allegiance. When Principal Earnshaw announced on Wednesday morning that "today's pledge will be recited by Evan Temple, one of our newest students," my ears perked up. We stood. We put our hands on our hearts.

Sometimes the kids on the PA system sound nervous and shaky, but Evan sounded like his usual self. We recited along with him. When he said "liberty and justice for all," we all sat down, but suddenly Evan's voice *did* get shaky. You never expect to hear anything after "liberty and justice for all," but this morning Evan said, "I would like to announce that Gretchen Scott's purse was found in the quad this morning behind the vending machine. It was not stolen as was previously reported. Thank—"

The microphone made a screeching sound, and I heard a muffled reprimand before the PA system clicked off.

Mr. Ted stared at the speaker, confused. "That was anomalous," he said.

Everyone looked at me. Braden scribbled something in his notebook and held it up for me to see. It said: *You're still a dog-eater.*

When the bell rang, I was the first one out the door.

Evan was leaning against my locker, blowing at his bangs.

"Oh my god," I said. "I can't believe you did that. Are you in trouble?"

"I was told I would never be allowed to say the pledge again." He moved aside so I could get to my locker. "I told them I would find a way to survive."

"How did that even happen?"

"I was in the office, turning in my form for MAYBO, and I—"

"Wait." I stopped turning the combination on my lock. "You were turning in your form for *what?*"

"The Model Airplane Youth Builders Organization. The club I was telling you about. The one I wanna start."

"That's kinda a long name, isn't it?"

"That's why I call it MAYBO."

"Why didn't you just name it the Model Airplane Builders Club?"

"Because M-A-B-C doesn't spell anything."

"Neither does M-A-Y-B-O."

He sighed as I opened my locker. "Look, do you wanna hear the story or not?" He continued. "I was turning in my form for my *awesomely named club* MAYBO, and a kid came in to turn Gretchen's purse in to the lost and found. One of the secretaries recognized it. She said it was the third time this year that someone had turned it in. Apparently the zombie bride is an airhead—those are my words—anyway, they were about to do the morning announcements, and I just got the idea to clear your name. Somebody had to do it. So I asked if I could do the pledge. I told Principal Earnshaw I was having trouble fitting in as a new kid, and it would be a good way to get my name out there."

"And he believed you?"

"Of course. I can be very charming."

Evan and I made our way down the south hall. I'm not sure why—maybe just to prove a point, to make myself feel better, or to give her a chance to apologize—but I walked right up to Gretchen's locker. She and Alyssa were chatting, but when we approached, they stopped talking. I kept my eyes on Gretchen.

"I'm glad they found your purse," I said. "I told you I didn't take it."

Gretchen opened her mouth, but Alyssa held up her index finger and cut her off.

"Whatever, Apple," she said. "How do we know that your freakish boyfriend didn't plant it behind that vending machine for you? I heard he was in the office when the purse was 'found.' Sounds suspicious to me. I still wouldn't trust you around any of my stuff." She pulled her own purse close to her hip.

"If that's what you need to believe to feel better about yourself, then go ahead," said Evan. He pulled my arm gently.

"Aw, Klepto and Freakboy make such a great couple, don't they?" Alyssa called after us.

"So much for clearing my name," I said.

"The people who matter know you're innocent," said Evan.

"But that's just you and me."

"Exactly."

The tardy bell was about to ring. I could tell by the way the hallway was thinning out. Before Evan and I turned the corner, I said, "My mom's having a friend over tonight. You can come over for dinner if you want. But just a warning—she's making fish." I pinched my nose.

"Great. I love fish," Evan said.

I spotted Lance and Jake coming toward us down the hallway. Over the past week or so, I had developed keen Lance-Jake-Braden-Alyssa radar. It worked really well too.

They didn't slow down, and for a second I thought they were going to ignore us. No such luck. Lance started barking. The barks were low and snippy at first, but then they got louder, like he was trying to sound like a German shepherd or a Doberman. Jake laughed like an idiot.

Before Evan and I could react, they'd turned the corner.

"We don't really eat dog," I said to Evan quietly.

"I know," he replied.

21. Guwapo

2FS4N: "The Ballad of John and Yoko"

When Evan came over, the first thing I wanted to do was properly introduce him to George, John, Ringo, and Paul. We went into my room, and I turned on *The White Album*. We had to leave the door open, because my mother said I wasn't allowed to have Evan in my room with the door closed. He sat on the floor with his back against the foot of my bed and looked at my poster of Matt Costa, but I could tell he wasn't really-really looking at it. He was listening to my mom speak Cebuano on the phone with Lita. I couldn't understand everything she was saying, but it sounded like she was asking her to bring something sweet for dessert.

"When you talk to your mom, do you speak your language or do you speak English?" asked Evan.

"English, mostly," I said, sitting down on the floor too.

"Why?"

"Because. We're in America. What's the point?"

"Because it's where you're from. Who cares if you're in America? Everyone can still speak different languages. It'd be boring if everyone spoke just one. Middle-earth didn't have just one language. There were tons. The dwarves even had secret languages inside their languages."

"I'll stick with English. I don't want to make myself any more of a freak than I already am. It's bad enough that people are saying I'm a . . . dog-eater."

Even though we both already knew that, it was embarrassing to think it, much less say it out loud.

"People are stupid sometimes," said Evan quietly. "All I know is, I wish I could speak another language."

"Well . . . I could teach you some words. Maybe not curse words, but real words."

Evan's face lit up in a wide smile. "Cool. Like what?"

I looked around the room. My eyes finally settled on Matt Costa again—holding his acoustic guitar and smiling down on both of us. Matt Costa is a singer from California. He's written a lot of really good songs, like "Sunshine" and "Mr. Pitiful."

"Matt Costa is *guwapo*," I said.

Evan repeated it. "What's that mean?"

"It means 'Matt Costa is handsome.'"

Evan stuck out his tongue like he'd just tasted something really gross. "Uh, if you're going to teach me Cebuano, you're gonna have to teach me much better stuff than that!"

I laughed.

"What's so great about Matt Costa?" asked Evan, motioning toward the poster. "He looks kinda goofy, if you ask me."

"I don't think so. Besides, I don't really care what he looks like. He's super talented and has a good sense of humor."

"How do you know he has a good sense of humor?"

"I can tell by his music."

"So you would date Quasimodo if he could play the guitar and had a good sense of humor?"

"Who is Quasimodo?"

"The hunchback of Notre Dame."

I shrugged. "I don't know. Maybe. He'd have to be really funny though. And he'd have to play the guitar better than anyone who ever lived. Better than George Harrison."

We sat there through four songs, with me drumming along with my hands and Evan staring into the corner of my room, chewing on his nail, deep in thought. By the time the music stopped, Lita had arrived and my mother was calling us so she could meet Evan.

"Hey, Mom," I said as we walked into the kitchen. *"Mangaon ta."* Evan nodded at me and grinned knowingly.

My mother looked too confused to respond. She hadn't heard me speak our language in a long time. She raised her eyebrows at Evan.

"I said 'let's eat,'" I explained to Evan.

"So you're Apple's friend!" said Lita. She was holding a big bag of defrosted fish; it looked like a sack of gray slime with eyes. My mother, who was wearing her Mabuhay Philippines! apron, took the bag and plopped it into the sink.

"What does *maboo-hay* mean?" asked Evan.

"Means 'Long live the Philippines!'" said my mother. *"Mabuhay! Mabuhay!"*

Then Lita joined in. *"Mabuhay* Philippines!"

This would normally be one of those times when

I'd wish to turn into a blackbird and fly away, but then Evan waved his open hands in the air and shouted *"Mabuhay!"* too. Then he launched into a series of fish-related questions as he watched my mother. Do you eat the eyes? What's all that slime? How do you cook these things?

As far as I was concerned, a fish should be battered and deep-fried, not cooked in its own skin on top of the stove.

When my mother finished hacking off the heads, she washed her hands for a long time. She has this obsession with clean hands, I guess because she's a nurse.

Evan picked up a fish by its tail and examined it closely.

"This is pretty gross," he said. "Good thing my mom's not here."

"Why?" I asked.

"She's a vegetarian. She would be pretty upset to see fish getting their heads chopped off." He dropped the fish back on the pile of its headless friends.

My mom turned off the faucet and dried her hands on a dish towel. "When I was a little girl, we ate lots of rice, fish, and vegetables. And we got haircuts," she said, flicking at Evan's hair playfully.

"And we ate plantains," Lita added. "What about your father, Evan? Does he eat meat?"

Evan nodded. "It drives my mom crazy, but he does it anyway. She says, 'Don't you know you're eating a living, breathing being?' And he looks at his fork and says, 'It looks pretty dead to me.' Then he eats it. When I'm home, my mom makes me eat what she cooks, but she lets me eat what I want at school. My dad says that doesn't count anyway, because school lunch is made of mystery meat."

I imagined Evan and his parents sitting around the dinner table—his dad slicing into a juicy steak, his mom fussing and smelling like the art room, and Evan talking about books and airplanes.

I wondered what it was like to have a complete family.

22. The Chapel Spring Voice Sensation

2FS4N: "Ob-La-Di, Ob-La-Da"

There are only a few small things I remember about the Philippines, but my mom used to say that, when we first moved to America, I would tell her that I missed home, especially the ocean.

"When you say something out loud, it makes it a big truth. Best to keep it in your mind and keep it small," she'd say.

The Dog Log was a spoken thing, something out

loud that was more real to me than anything else, even more real than my father, since the idea of him felt far away like the Philippines. But the one thing that made the Dog Log a little less real was the fact that it was banned from school and there was no written copy of it—no piece of paper for everyone to see. So I could kind of pretend that the list didn't exist, that I wasn't on it, or that no one knew about it.

Until the following Tuesday morning.

Braden strode into homeroom as always—like he was making a grand entrance—with his phone in his hand. He walked over to Claire Hathaway and showed her something on the screen. It was clear that they'd had a conversation before, because he was saying, "See? You're on the list. Told you." Claire's cheeks turned pink. I glanced down at my notebook and pretended I wasn't listening. I couldn't help listening though.

When Claire giggled, I knew they couldn't be talking about the Dog Log. And there was no way someone like Claire would be on the Dog Log anyway.

Danica Landry walked over to Claire and Braden. "What list?" she asked.

I propped my elbow up on my desk and rested my head in my hand so I could pretend I was studying something important instead of eavesdropping.

"The Hot Lot. We're starting a new tradition," said Braden. "It's a list of the hottest girls in school."

There was a pause, and I just knew Danica was scrolling through the list, probably hoping with all her might that she was included. I could tell that she wasn't, because pretty soon she started picking apart all the girls who were. Carol Anne Nelson's hair was too long. Nicole Rentrop's hair was too short. And then—

"How come *Gretchen Scott's* number one?" asked Danica. "She's not even pretty."

Gretchen, number one on this so-called "Hot Lot"? I wondered what Alyssa and Gretchen would think about that. I wasn't surprised—Gretchen *was* pretty—but the thought of a "Hot Lot" seemed way more stupid than a "Dog Log."

I wished I was on that list instead of the other one though.

"What's this second list?" asked Danica.

I felt trouble coming. And sure enough: "That's the Dog Log," said Braden.

The Dog Log was documented. Danica, Claire, and Braden started speaking in low voices. I heard a few hushed giggles. I felt them looking at me. My skin burned. They were reading my name, right there on Braden's phone. The entire list could be spread to everyone with the simple touch of a button.

Maybe that button had already been pushed.

When I saw Evan standing outside the library at lunch, practically bouncing out of his skin, I assumed he was going to tell me what I already knew: The Dog Log had been spread to every student at Chapel Spring Middle School, and I might as well be wearing an enormous flashing sign that said, Ugly Loser. But as soon as he saw me he smiled and grabbed my elbow.

"You gotta see this," he said.

"See what?" I followed him as he brisk-walked down the hall. "Where are we going?"

"Band room. You gotta see this—or better yet, you gotta *hear* this." As we got closer Evan slowed down and put his fingers to his lips. Then he gently pushed open the door.

It was amazing.

Singing. That's what it was.

Not just any singing though. Not singing like I heard from the swing choir or when Gretchen and Alyssa used to rehearse in front of me during lunch. This was *real* singing. This was deep, powerful, booming singing. It sounded like an adult. Maybe it *was* an adult. I couldn't tell. Evan and I crept toward Mr. Z's office, because that was where it was coming from.

"Look," Evan whispered, pointing through a thin sliver in the blinds.

I saw Mr. Z sitting on the corner of his desk with a guitar, and standing there was the last person

I ever expected to see—Heleena Moffett. This big, quiet mouse walked up and down the halls every day without saying much of anything. Every time she spoke, it sounded small, like a squeak, but there was nothing small about her voice now.

My mouth dropped open. I glanced at Evan.

He blew at his hair. "I know, right?"

"Where'd she learn to sing like that?"

"I don't know."

He chewed his finger and listened as I squinted through the blinds and watched. When she stopped a few minutes later, I tugged Evan's sleeve.

"Come on. Let's go," I said.

"No, let's wait," he said.

"What do you mean, wait?" I said. "I don't want them to know we're here."

"Why not? It's not like we heard anything bad. We heard something the opposite of bad. We heard something amazingly awe—"

Mr. Z's door opened wide, and Heleena stepped

out. She looked just as quiet and shy as ever. When she saw us, her eyes got real big and her cheeks turned pink. She didn't smile.

Mr. Z did though.

"Hey!" he said. "What a surprise. Ready for a lesson, Apple?"

"No," I said, glancing at Heleena. "You told me you were busy on Tuesdays. I was planning to come, uh, another day, but—"

"No, she wasn't," Evan said. "She hasn't come by because she doesn't have her own guitar, and she doesn't want to ask you to borrow one."

Now *my* face turned red. I swatted Evan's shoulder.

He shrugged. "It's true."

Mr. Z crossed his arms, still smiling. "So the truth comes out. Well, at least you were right about Tuesdays. Heleena has voice lessons. Although I'm not sure who the real teacher is."

Heleena's cheeks turned an even deeper shade of pink.

"How'd you learn to sing like that?" Evan asked her. "Just from coming to voice lessons with Mr. Z?"

"Ha!" Mr. Z said as Heleena looked at her feet. "You don't learn how to sing like that by just taking lessons. It comes naturally. Some people are born to do certain things. Lessons only help make your talent shine even brighter." He turned to Heleena and smiled proudly. "Heleena was born with a big voice."

Evan looked at me. "Maybe you were born to play guitar and write songs."

"Maybe," Mr. Z agreed. "There's only one way to find out." He disappeared into his office. When he came back a few seconds later, he was holding a Yamaha guitar. It wasn't the Fender Starcaster I'd always wanted, but it was something to strum, and here he was, holding it out to me. "Take this home and see how it feels."

My heart was beating really fast—but this time I wasn't scared. I was too busy looking at the guitar. It was used but in good shape. Some parts were scuffed, and it wasn't very shiny at all, but I didn't care. I studied the strings and wondered how many songs had been played on it. There was even a strap, though the leather was worn and the thread had unraveled in places.

"Try it," said Evan.

I slipped it over my shoulder and adjusted the strap so I could play and hold the guitar at the same time. I asked Mr. Z if I was doing everything right, and he said I was.

"It suits you, Apple," he said. "Fool around on it. See how you do."

Evan, Heleena, and I walked out of the band room together. The guitar felt natural and light on my back. I shoved my hands in my pockets. I felt like Sheryl Crow or Tracy Chapman.

"How long have you been taking lessons?" I asked Heleena. "You don't even sound like you need them. You have the most amazing voice I've ever heard. It's definitely one of your IFs."

"What's an IF?" she asked.

"I believe that there are at least three interesting facts about every person on Earth," I said as we made our way down the hall. "I call them IFs."

"That's a good theory," Heleena said. "What are your IFs, Apple?"

Before I could answer, we heard a strange sound coming down the hallway.

It was barking.

Jake, Braden, Lance, and a few other boys were clustered near the water fountain, and I guess they'd seen us coming. They cupped their mouths with their hands, ducked their heads, and howled.

Everyone was looking at us. Some kids were laughing; others just stared.

I wondered if Heleena knew they were barking at both of us. I wondered if she knew about the Dog Log. I couldn't tell by her expression. She was looking down at her feet.

23. How to Deliver a Secret Guitar

2FS4N: "A Hard Day's Night"

In a big city you have to know how to get around. That's why I needed maps of New Orleans. Lots and lots of maps that showed places to eat and places to stay. I printed them from online. The city looked more complicated than I thought, but I would learn. And besides, I wasn't planning on leaving the French Quarter that much. I could play all day, earn money, and find a place to sleep. I would make my own life, just like George Harrison and all the other great musicians did.

Getting Mr. Z's guitar into the house would be impossible without my mother seeing, so Evan and I made a plan that involved me giving the Yamaha to him and then him delivering it to me through my bedroom window after dark. It's not like guitars are easy to hide. After that I would shove towels under my door or turn the volume on my music up, so that she wouldn't hear me practice.

At ten o'clock that night, I was sitting right next to my window, staring out at the lawn. Even though I'd been in this room almost my entire life, I'd never really sat and looked out the window before. There's something eerie about nighttime, especially when you're looking at it through your window. I heard a dog bark somewhere in the distance, which reminded me of the barking that afternoon at school.

I wondered what nighttime in New Orleans would look like.

Then Evan showed up, my guitar strapped to his back. Pretty soon I could hear his bicycle tires pushing down on the grass and twigs, and there he was, on the other side of my window. He had a big smile on his face; I could tell that he was excited about breaking out in the middle of the night. Well, it was only ten thirty, but it may as well have been the middle of the night.

I slid up the window some more. Evan handed me the guitar.

"Thanks," I whispered, leaning it against the wall. My heart was beating fast again. Even though I wasn't the one who had broken out of my house, it was kind of exciting knowing that Evan and I were sharing a secret.

"No problem," he said. He wrapped both hands around the handlebars of his bike. "You deserve it."

My cheeks got warm, but I wasn't really sure why. It wasn't often that I got embarrassed around Evan.

I reached into my pocket and pulled out the list I'd made for him earlier that night.

"What's this?" he whispered. He unfolded it and squinted at the words in the glow of the streetlight.

"Some Cebuano phrases. You know, if you still want to learn them."

"Cool," said Evan. He tried to read a few of them aloud, but it was too hard to see the words clearly in the darkness. Then he pulled an envelope out of his back pocket and handed it to me. "I have something for you too."

The envelope held something small. I couldn't tell what it was.

"Don't open it until I leave," he said.

"What is it?" I asked.

"You'll see," he said, smiling. He folded the list of Cebuano words and put it in his pocket. Then he stood up on one pedal. "I'd better go before I get busted."

"Okay."

I expected him to take off in a hurry, but he stayed a few seconds longer, holding on to his handlebars and looking at me like he was waiting for something to happen. Just when I was about to ask if he wanted to tell me something, he smiled and said, "Good night, Apple."

"It's Analyn," I whispered, smiling.

"Yeah, right."

I watched him pedal slowly away. I watched until he disappeared down the dark street. Then I sat on my rug and opened the envelope.

It was a guitar pick. I turned it around in my fingers. It was bright, shiny, and gold.

The first time I plucked the strings, it was louder than I expected, so I wedged the towel under the door even more tightly and moved to the back right corner of my room. I kept the lights off to avoid suspicion.

I didn't know how to play anything, so of course I just picked at the strings and tried out their different sounds. I listened to the sounds the strings made when I held them down on the neck and the sounds they made when I didn't. I tried as many chords as I could remember from the book and from online.

I got my laptop and watched a video of "Blackbird" for the dozenth time, but it was hard to keep up with the chords. Maybe I needed to be sitting across from Mr. Z.

I thought about the poster of the Beatles on his wall.

I'd bet anything he knew how to play "Blackbird."

24. Blackbird Fly

2FS4N: "Get Back"

When I met Evan at his locker the next morning, Heleena was already there. It was a strange sight, only because I'd never really seen Heleena talk to anyone at school before. She wasn't really talking now either, because Evan was blabbing endlessly, but she was listening and nodding and even smiling a little. A shy smile.

"Hey, guys," I said as I walked up. It felt good

to have Heleena there, but I wasn't sure why. Maybe because I knew she needed a friend—and I did too.

"*Hola,*" said Evan. He shut his locker. "*Kumusta ka?*"

"It's kah-moo-stah-kah, not kah-moostay," I corrected.

"Kah-moo-stah-kah?"

Heleena raised her eyebrows at us.

"Evan is learning my native language," I explained. "He asked how I was doing."

"That's neat," Heleena said.

"I know a curse word," Evan added. Then he shook his fists in the air and said, "*Atsara! Atsara!*"

"What's it mean?" asked Heleena.

"We don't know," Evan and I said in unison.

He turned to me. "I was saying how awesome it would be if you learned some Beatles songs on the guitar and Heleena could sing them while you play. Like a duo. And I could be your manager. Maybe I could book you some gigs." He snapped his fingers.

"You can play at the inaugural meeting of MAYBO."

"What's MAYBO?" asked Heleena.

"It's the new school club I'm starting."

Heleena looked terrified. "I don't think I could sing in front of a group."

"That's okay, because I'm the only member," said Evan.

"It doesn't matter anyway, because I don't know how to play anything yet," I said. "I watched some videos last night, but I'm having trouble with 'Blackbird' because I've got to play a D and then have my middle finger on the G and then my ring finger on the B fret and open with a—"

Evan put up his hand. "My head just exploded."

Heleena said she needed to go to her locker before homeroom, so we followed her. I tried not to think about who we might find lurking around it.

"You may not be able to play it yet, but you will," said Evan, turning to me. Quietly he asked, "Did you open the envelope?"

"Yes." I showed him my fingertips. My index finger and thumb were both red and raw.

Evan beamed.

I smelled Gretchen's shampoo before I heard Alyssa's voice. "He told me that I was in the discussion, and if there were a list of the top fifteen, I definitely would've been on there."

"I think it's all stupid," said Gretchen.

"Easy for you to say, big number one!" said Alyssa, smiling as she playfully swatted Gretchen's arm.

When we reached Heleena's locker, Gretchen glanced at us over Alyssa's shoulder. Alyssa turned around.

"Wow, it's some kind of Dog Log convention at Big-leena's locker, I see," she said.

"Whatever," I said.

Alyssa looked at me. "Gretchen is number one on the Hot Lot. That's something, huh?"

I shrugged and shifted my eyes to Gretchen. "Yeah, I guess. Congratulations?"

"Those lists don't mean anything," said Gretchen. She wasn't smiling.

"All the boys were whistling at her yesterday after school," said Alyssa. She giggled. "It was so embarrassing, because I was walking right there with her and they *wouldn't stop*."

"How mature," said Evan.

Alyssa crossed her arms. "The girls need to make a list for the guys so I can put *you* on the Dog Log."

Evan bit his fingernails, pretending to be scared. "No, no, not the Dog Log! How will I survive?"

I caught Heleena smiling again.

"Freak," said Alyssa.

"I've got you on a list, Evil Dorothy. You wanna know what it is?"

Alyssa sighed as if she couldn't be bothered with the conversation any longer, especially since it'd backfired on her. "Let's go, Gretchen," she said, grabbing Gretchen's arm. "Bye-bye, doggies."

Heleena opened her locker and grabbed some books.

"Don't worry about them," Evan said. "Their brains aren't fully developed."

"I'm used to it," said Heleena. She glanced at me and looked away. "It's okay."

And then I realized: She was used to it from me too. I had been on the other side of the locker. Part of that group. I'd never said anything directly to her, but I was there and walked alongside Alyssa and listened to her gossip and laughed at the things she said. I wasn't mean like Alyssa, but I'd stood there silently.

In some ways, maybe that's worse.

It had taken me fifteen minutes to sneak out of the house that morning with the guitar. I had ridden my bike to school so my mom wouldn't see it, which is something I hadn't done since last year when Alyssa told me my bike was "fantastically crappy." Wearing the Yamaha on my back meant I couldn't carry a backpack, so I had to carry my books in the crook of my arm. It made my arms tired, but it was worth it.

When we got to the band room, Mr. Z was sitting in one of the orchestra chairs, reading.

"Hello, Mr. Temple, Miss Moffett, and Miss Yengko!" he said cheerfully. He closed his book. "Are you all here for lessons?" A guitar was on the seat next to him. He picked it up.

"No. Just Apple," said Evan.

"We're only here for moral support," added Heleena.

"Ah, like an entourage." He moved a chair to face him. The legs screeched against the floor. He told me to sit, so I did. "So tell me, Apple. Is there any particular kind of music you like, or—"

"The Beatles," the three of us said in unison.

"Great. The Beatles. Perfect place to start. We can start with a few simple chords and then we can—"

"I want to play 'Blackbird,'" I said. "And 'Here Comes the Sun.'"

"Oh. Well, you should probably learn a few simple chords first. Within the next few months, you'll probably be able to play some Beatles. Depending on how everything goes."

"But—" I glanced at Evan. "Is it possible to learn just the songs on their own, so it doesn't take a few months?" Quickly I added, "I'm just really excited."

Mr. Z frowned. "Playing the guitar takes a lot of patience. You have to be sure you're serious before you commit."

"She's serious," said Evan.

Heleena nodded.

"Besides, Mr. Z," Evan continued, "we're ready to start our band." He motioned among the three of us and turned to Heleena. "Do you think you could sing 'Blackbird' and 'Here Comes the Sun' if Apple learned how to play them?"

She shrugged. "I've never heard them before."

"Heleena can sing anything," said Mr. Z. "But learning a musical instrument is—"

"Apple can do it," Heleena said.

Mr. Z pressed his lips together and looked at me. "We can try, Apple, but keep in mind, it takes most people months just to figure out the chords, and then it takes years to really master playing songs. You're supposed to start off small, and learn how to fingerpick, before you try to take on titans like the Beatles. We can just go in like gangbusters if you want, but if it doesn't work out, you have to trust me and listen. Deal?"

"Deal," I said.

"We're leaving," said Heleena to Evan. "Lessons are better when you don't have any distractions." She tugged Evan's sleeve.

When they were gone, Mr. Z positioned his guitar. I did too.

"All right then," he said. "Let's play."

In fourth grade, I knew a girl named Laurel Griffin. Laurel was kind of like Lita's daughter Olivia—she made straight As, always knew the answers in class, never got sent to the office, that kind of thing. To make matters worse, Laurel played concert violin. She started playing violin at the age of three. She didn't even have to learn the chords; she just picked up the violin and played a concerto. The reason I know all this is because Laurel told everyone at least twice a day. She would say things like: "Jack Hamilton may have won the spelling bee, but I'm a child prodigy!" or "My parents say I should have my hands insured, because I'm a child prodigy in concert violin, and if anything happens to my fingers, it will be a tragedy."

The funny thing is, Laurel wasn't known for being a child prodigy. Instead she was known for being a bragger.

One afternoon at recess, instead of running off straight to the slide or the jungle gym, she'd stretched, yawned, and plopped down on the grass.

"I'm so tired," she'd said, even though no one had

asked. She'd said it loudly so we could hear. "I was up all night practicing for my upcoming concert. Dad says it's not really practicing, since I play perfectly every time, but he still makes me play it over and over. He's simply impossible." That was one of her favorite phrases. "Anyway, I'm so tired. . . ."

Laurel Griffin annoyed everyone so much that she had no friends, and she annoyed me to the point that I promised myself I would never become a bragger. Then again, I never had anything to brag about.

Not until my lesson with Mr. Z.

Ten minutes into it, he narrowed his eyes and said, "Are you sure you've never played?"

"Last night was the first time I picked up a guitar."

"Then how do you know all the chords?"

"Well, I don't know *all* of them. Just some of them."

"Most of them."

"Okay," I said, smiling. "Most of them, I guess."

"So how do you know them?"

I stretched my right hand. Playing the guitar can give you hand and finger cramps.

"I read about them," I said. "And I watched some videos. Before I ever got the guitar." I looked down at the borrowed Yamaha.

He shook his head. "I've never seen anyone learn a musical instrument that way. I've never heard of anyone just being able to pick up a guitar and play it. Except maybe Jimi Hendrix." He tilted his head. "Your father isn't Jimi Hendrix, is he?"

"Not unless Jimi Hendrix lived in the Philippines and played *Abbey Road* on an old tape player."

Mr. Z laughed, then said, "Let's try something." He patted his guitar. "I'll play a song." He pointed at me. "You watch me and listen. Then we'll see if you can play it back."

"Can you play 'Blackbird'?"

He nodded.

"Okay," I said. I fixed my eyes on his hands.

"Ready?"

I nodded without moving my eyes.

I watched him play, and even though I was concentrating really hard, I could still hear the song in my head. I'd listened to it so many times, it was a part of me. That's how it goes with favorite songs sometimes.

When he finished, I sat up straight and got myself ready.

"Do you think you can play it?" he asked. "Just from that?"

I pressed my lips together. "Yes. I think so."

And I did.

Twice.

25. Goddess of Guitar

2FS4N: "Eight Days a Week"

I carried Mr. Z's guitar everywhere.

In homeroom, the week before our field trip, Claire Hathaway asked if she could hold it. She strummed a few strings.

"This is cool," she said.

Braden snickered. "She probably lifted it from Mr. Z," he said. But either no one heard or no one paid attention.

When Danica saw Claire playing the guitar, she asked if she could try it too.

"Do you really know how to play this?" she asked.

I strummed the opening bars of "Blackbird." Then Danica and Claire both tried, but it sounded like a bunch of jumbled chords.

"It's harder than it looks," said Danica.

But it hadn't been. Not for me.

Even Mr. Ted had something to say when he came in and saw the three of us gathered around the guitar.

"Well, well, it looks like there is a musician in our midst," he said. "Perhaps one morning you could regale us in song!"

Claire, Danica, and I exchanged grins and giggled. Mr. Ted laughed.

After second period I met Evan and Heleena at Heleena's locker. I had my guitar on my back, and I didn't care if Alyssa was there or not. Turns out she wasn't. It was just Gretchen, shoving books into her neatly organized locker by herself.

"Hey, Apple," she said quietly.

I thought about ignoring her, but I didn't.

"Hey, Gretchen," I said, turning to Evan when he nudged me.

"I wonder if they'll let you take the guitar on the field trip," he said.

I'd been wondering that same thing for days and days. I needed it—or at least I needed to raise the money to buy my own. Time was running out.

Heleena reached into her locker and pulled out a Ziploc bag full of coins. She handed it to me.

"For the Apple Yengko Fender Starcaster Donation Fund," she said.

"Wow," I said. The bag was heavy with quarters, dimes, nickels, and pennies.

"I had a bunch of loose change, and I wasn't using it for anything, so I figured . . ."

Evan nudged me and smiled.

"This is great, Heleena," I said. I reached over

and hugged her. "Pretty soon I'll be able to give Mr. Z his Yamaha back and get a guitar of my own."

The three of us walked together to our next class, but it almost felt like there were four of us now, with the Yamaha. No one else at school carried a guitar. It was starting to feel like an extension of my body. I couldn't wait until I got one of my own. I wondered what I would name it. Musicians always name their guitars.

The next time I saw Gretchen, she was alone again. I knew Alyssa wasn't out sick, because I'd already seen her walking with Claire Hathaway. I wondered if Alyssa and Gretchen were in some kind of argument. I figured I would never find out, but just before my lesson with Mr. Z, I went into the bathroom outside the band room and there was Gretchen, standing in the corner with her back against the wall. Her eyes were red and puffy, and she was holding a wad of toilet paper. She looked surprised to see me, and I couldn't blame her—hardly anyone ever used this girls' bathroom unless the band was practicing. It looked forgotten too. Some of the stalls were missing doors, and one of the mirrors was cracked.

"Um . . . hey," I said.

She wiped her face in a hurry and shoved the tissue in her pocket, probably along with some Skittles wrappers and other things.

"Are you okay?" I asked.

She smiled. Tears still glistened on her cheeks. She wiped them away. "Yeah, sure." She walked over to the mirrors and examined her face.

I didn't move from my spot. "Did you and Alyssa have a fight or something?"

"She accused me of kissing Jake. As if I would kiss that . . . that . . . *pig*." Her voice sounded funny, probably because of all the crying.

"Why would you do that? She knows you like Lance and that Lance likes you."

"Not anymore." She went into a stall and got another wad of toilet paper.

"What happened?"

"He said Jake's been telling everyone we made out. I don't know why Jake would ever say that."

"Because he's a jerk."

Gretchen nodded. She was standing in front of the mirror that was cracked, so her face looked distorted and rearranged. She threw the tissue at her reflection.

"I hate Alyssa," she said.

"I know how you feel."

She looked down at the sink. Her brown hair fell off her shoulders and shielded her face.

"I hate Jake too," she said.

"Lance should've believed you," I said. "So he's an idiot too."

She lifted her head. "You're right," she said. "I guess I just hate everyone."

She laughed lightly. I did too.

"Except you, of course," she added.

I adjusted the guitar on my shoulder and walked toward the door.

"Call me if you need me," I said. "We can hate everyone together."

Just before I walked out, Gretchen said, "Apple?"

I propped open the door with my right Chuck and turned around. "Yeah?"

She didn't look up. "I'm sorry about the purse thing. I never really thought you took it."

"I know. You just misplaced it because you're forgetful. It's one of your three IFs, remember?" I smiled. Suddenly I felt terrible for Gretchen.

"What are my other two?" she asked.

"You keep Skittles wrappers in your pockets," I said. "And you always smell like shampoo."

She laughed.

I let the door swing shut behind me.

★ ★ ★

Evan came over that evening to secretly pass my Yamaha through the window and have dinner with me and my mom.

"Kumusta ka?" he asked, and my mother said she was fine. Then he tried to ask what was for dinner but he failed miserably, because my mother was never able to understand what he was really asking. Finally he sighed and said, "What's for dinner? Filipino food?"

My mother laughed. "How about pizza?"

"Pepperoni," I said.

"Pepperoni," Evan agreed. As my mother nodded and riffled through her purse for her phone he turned to me and said, "I bet the food is gonna be the only good thing about the field trip next week."

"Shh," I said, widening my eyes. *"Shh."*

What? Evan mouthed.

"Field trip?" asked my mother, still looking in her purse. "Is there a field trip?"

"Only for Evan's class." I tugged his arm. "Let's go wait for the pizza outside."

Once we were sitting on the back porch I explained that I never gave my mother the field-trip permission slip.

"I forged her signature," I said.

"Why?"

"I knew she'd want to go as a chaperone."

"Oh."

We sat on the edge of the porch. Evan rubbed the heels of his sneakers into the grass and chewed on his fingernail. "Apple, can I ask you something?"

"Yeah."

In the span of a few seconds, I imagined every question he could ever ask, everything from *Can I kiss you?* to *How does it feel to be the third-ugliest girl in school?* but then he asked the one question I never expected:

"How come you don't like your mom?"

The question surprised me so much that a little gasp caught in my throat.

"It's not like I hate her or anything," I said.

For once in his life, Evan didn't have anything

else to say. I didn't either. We both just sat there and watched his sneakers make a faint trail in the grass. I turned his question over and over in my head. Evan thought I hated my mother. I wondered if she thought that too.

"What was wrong with Gretchen today?" he finally asked.

"Jake Bevans told everyone they made out."

I looked at my crappy bike and my weekend backpack, which was perched up next to it. I hadn't been anywhere with that weekend backpack for a while. Ever since the Dog Log, I'd spent most of my time in my room, listening to music, playing the guitar, planning my escape, and thinking about the Dog Log. I thought back to the day I'd gone to Alyssa's party.

"I wonder if Jake told people they made out because Gretchen was first on that list," I said. I leaned back on my hands. "Just to make himself look good."

Evan pulled up a handful of grass and tossed it. "Probably. He's an idiot."

There was no arguing with that.

"Ugh," I said. "I can't imagine making out with Jake Bevans."

"Me neither."

I giggled and smacked Evan's shoulder.

"I'm serious," I said. "He's disgusting. They all are."

"We should come up with some kind of list of our own. Something to pass around school that has all their names on it. Like, the People Who Suck List."

"Nah. I think two lists are enough."

"Yeah, you're probably right." A cardinal chirped and landed in a tree nearby. Evan stared at it.

"Oh, I almost forgot to tell you," he said. "Someone else joined MAYBO."

"Really?" I didn't mean to sound so surprised. "Who?"

"Brian Watkins. Do you know him?"

"Yeah. He's the guy who wears those bright yellow high-tops, right?"

"I don't know. I've never met him. I only know his name, because I stopped by the office to ask if anyone signed up."

"I'll point him out to you at school."

"Bright yellow high-tops shouldn't be hard to miss."

My mom opened the back door with the phone in her hand.

"Apple, come talk to the pizza," she said, waving her phone at me.

I grumbled but got up and took the phone from her.

The man on the other end of the line said, "Hello? I need someone who speaks English. *English.*" His voice was loud and irritated. There was a spattering of laughter in the background; I could hear it clearly, because the phone was turned up so loud. I looked at my mother and turned down the volume. I heard him say, "Sometimes I forget I'm even in America. You should have to be able to at least speak the language before you come to this country. Jesus."

"I can," I said. "And so can she."

"Excuse me?"

"I said, I do speak English, and so does my mother."

"Well, it wasn't clear." Abruptly he said, "Go ahead with your order now."

I looked at Evan and my mother. She looked down at him on the porch and said something about not having good English.

"I try, but sometimes they don't understand me." And she smiled.

I knew that smile. It was the kind of smile that wants to run away from your face. It's the kind of smile you give when your so-called friends are making fun of you or sitting quietly while someone else is. It was the way I smiled at Alyssa's party. The way I had smiled for months.

I could see Jake Bevans in my mind. He was holding his eyes back to make slits and talking about dog-eaters and hot dogs, and now, as I looked at my mother with her runaway smile and listened to the sighs and laughter in the pizzeria, I felt my chest tighten.

"Hello? Hello?" said the pizza man.

"Maybe you weren't listening," I said.

"What?"

My mother and Evan exchanged confused glances.

"Maybe she *was* speaking English, and you weren't listening!"

I turned off the phone before he could say anything else and handed it back to my mother.

"Mangaon ta," I said.

"What happened with the pizza?" she asked, her eyebrows raised.

"We can eat our own good food at home. Besides, it's cheaper, right?"

My mother reached over and pinched my cheek like I was a five-year-old.

"Maybe you're not turning American after all!" she said.

After she went back into the house, Evan stood up and asked, "What does maang-aah-ohn mean?"

"It means 'Let's eat *pancit*.'" And I motioned for him to follow me into the house for dinner.

26. Sometimes People Need a Serenade

2FS4N: "Dear Prudence"

"Gretchen Scott is a dirty troll."

The sentence was there in big black marker on the wall of the girls' bathroom—not the old bathroom by the band room but the one in the main hall, the one that everyone used. It was written as big as ever and was so unexpected that I took a step back and read it again. I felt like I'd been socked in the gut and, what's worse, I knew Alyssa didn't write it, because it wasn't her handwriting.

The storm against Gretchen was spreading.

I worked my way through the crowd of girls by the sink, dampened a paper towel, and went back to the wall to wash it off, but all I did was wipe away bathroom grime and make the black permanent marker stand out even more. I tossed the wet paper towel in the trash and tried to scrape off the words with my fingernail, but it didn't do any good. Finally I gave up and walked to homeroom, where I found out what "dirty troll" meant.

According to Danica, who was talking to Claire, Gretchen had made out with at least twelve boys since the beginning of the school year.

"It's a *fact* too," Danica said. She leaned over and acted like she was talking quietly, but everyone nearby could hear her. "Four of the guys told me about it themselves, and it was *very detailed*, so they couldn't have made it up."

"That doesn't sound like something Gretchen would do," said Claire.

"Of course not," said Danica dismissively. "She plays this role like she's Miss Goody-Goody, but it's all fake."

I sighed and rolled my eyes at them, but they were so involved in their conversation that they didn't see.

When Braden came in, he immediately walked over to Claire and Danica. I'd noticed that he'd made a point to talk to Claire every single morning ever since she made it on the Hot Lot.

"I was just talking to Claire about Gretchen Scott," said Danica.

Braden sat on Claire's desk. "What, being number one on the list?" he said.

"No, not that," Danica said. She motioned for him to come closer, and he did. She whispered in his ear.

I glared at them.

"That isn't true," I said, from my desk. I had to speak up to make sure they heard me.

"How do you know?" Braden said. "Are you her babysitter or something?"

Danica laughed.

"Besides, no one can believe a thief. Especially one who eats Fido for supper," he added, throwing a few barks my way as an added bonus.

I rolled my eyes again as Mr. Ted came into the room and got everyone under control.

I thought about Gretchen. I wondered if she'd seen "Gretchen Scott is a dirty troll."

Even as Mr. Ted talked about next week's field trip and gave us reminders and used words like *excursion* and *promenade*, I kept thinking about her. I decided I'd talk to her when I met Heleena and Evan at our lockers, but I didn't see her anywhere after the bell rang.

"Did you see what was written about Gretchen in the girls' bathroom?" I asked Heleena.

"Yeah," Heleena said. She frowned.

"Whatever it was, she deserves it. Karma," said Evan.

"No, she doesn't," I said.

★ ★ ★

After school I rode my bike to her house. There were no cars in the driveway, so I figured her parents were at work. I've been friends with Gretchen for a couple years, but I've never met her parents. I don't think they're home very much.

Gretchen opened the door in a T-shirt and pajama pants. She wasn't wearing any makeup.

"Apple." She gave a runaway smile. "Hey."

"Hey."

"What are you doing here?"

"Are you okay?"

Her smile disappeared. She stepped aside and opened the door for me.

Her house always smelled like fresh potpourri. I'd been there only a few times, but I remembered that. Everything was neat and orderly. I followed her to the living room, where we both sat on the enormous, plush couch. I'd forgotten about that couch and how comfortable it was. I put my guitar on the carpet so I could get snug.

She lifted her feet and hugged one of the throw pillows.

"You weren't in school today," I said. "Are you sick?"

She turned down the volume on the television. "Not really. I just didn't feel that great." She stared at the now-mute guy on the screen.

"Are Alyssa and Lance still mad at you?"

"Everyone is. I don't know why. I didn't even do anything." Her voice cracked. She pressed her lips together real tight.

I thought about the bathroom wall.

"They're just jealous," I said. And even though I knew it was true, I also knew it probably wouldn't make her feel any better.

She kept staring at the silent television with her lips pressed tight.

I searched for words in my head, but I couldn't think of any good ones. Gretchen was searching for words too, I could tell, but I wasn't sure what words she wanted until she looked at me and said, "Apple?"

"Yeah?"

"You didn't deserve to be on the Dog Log."

"No one does."

She nodded. "Those lists are stupid."

"Very."

"Maybe we should come up with our own list."

"Evan said the same thing. At first I didn't think it was a great idea, but then I thought of a good one."

She smiled a little. "Really? What is it?"

"A song list." I reached down and picked up my guitar. "You wanna hear one?"

She smiled even wider. A real smile.

"Definitely," she said.

I sat up straight and tuned my guitar.

"Apple?" she said again.

"Yeah?"

"I think you're beautiful."

Under any other circumstances, we probably would have thought it was the cheesiest thing ever and giggled until we couldn't stop, but at that moment she found the perfect words for both of us.

"I think you are too," I said, and I pulled Evan's guitar pick out of my pocket.

I decided to play "Here Comes the Sun." Even though "Blackbird" is my all-time favorite Beatles song ever, "Here Comes the Sun" always cheers me up. Plus I'd just learned how to play it the night before.

It was the first time I ever played "Here Comes the Sun" in front of anyone, and it was the first time I ever sang in front of anyone except myself, but I didn't even feel embarrassed. I just strummed and sang and watched Gretchen giggle and listen and smile and tap her feet. I thought about them calling me a dog-eater. I thought about the Dog Log and "Gretchen is a dirty troll" and the Hot Lot and "Big-leena" and Jake Bevans. I thought about Alyssa in the fifth grade, and how sad and boring she was now that all she cared about was tiers and lists. I thought about the way Braden had laughed at the dance and about my mother and Evan. Everything rushed through my head, but then it all faded away into the back of my mind, and none of that stuff mattered because there was music.

27. Always Pick George

2FS4N: "Getting Better"

When Alyssa and I first became friends, we would meet at the park near our neighborhood and sail down the slides or see who could go the highest on the swing set or race from the east corner to the west. As other things became more important, like tiers and boys, we stopped going. It's funny how something can be a big part of your life, and then you can forget it's even there. That's how I felt about the park until the day Heleena and I decided to get together so we could rehearse. Heleena didn't want to practice at her house, and I didn't want to practice at mine, so after I left Gretchen's, I texted her to see if she wanted to meet under the red canopy near the basketball courts. I sat on top of the picnic table and played songs while I waited. I practiced "Oh! Darling" from *Abbey Road*. It's one of their more bluesy songs, so it wasn't the best acoustic tune, but I liked it.

I was on my fourth rendition when Heleena walked up. Her face was shiny with sweat, even though the sky was overcast. It's hot in Louisiana even when it's November and the sun is hiding.

"Are you practicing some new songs?" asked Heleena.

She sat on one of the benches instead of on the tabletop.

"Yeah. I'm trying all different ones, just to see what it's like."

"I do that too."

This was the first time Heleena and I had ever hung out alone, so it was kinda awkward. I plucked a few strings, and she watched me silently. The clouds shifted. It was darker than usual. It probably wasn't a good day to practice, but we needed to get some rehearsals in. Neither of us had any idea what performance we were rehearsing for, and I wasn't sure how this would help me in New Orleans, but it seemed like an important thing to do. Plus we had promised Evan.

"How did you learn to play the guitar so fast?" asked Heleena.

"I'm not sure," I said. "I just knew. Maybe because I couldn't stop thinking about it. Sometimes I even play in my sleep. Is that weird?"

"No."

I stopped plucking.

"What about you?" I asked. "Where'd you learn to sing?"

She thought about it for a second. "I'm not sure," she said. "I just knew."

We both smiled like we were sharing a secret. Maybe we were.

"I'm sorry about your friend, by the way," she said. "She seems really nice."

"Who, Alyssa?" I grinned.

Heleena laughed. Loud this time, not quiet like in the library.

Once we stopped laughing, I said, "It's so wrong what's going on with Gretchen, because she never did any of those things. They're just jealous. She gets put on some dumb list, and now she's an outcast."

Heleena pulled a loose sliver of wood off the table.

"Like us," she said.

We'd never talked about the Dog Log before. It was like this big umbrella that hovered over both of us, but we had never acknowledged it. Until now.

"Yeah," I said. "Like us."

"My mom says one day none of it will matter. Like, when we're out of school, we won't even remember stuff that happened in middle school or high school.

She says everyone will be busy living their own lives. But I don't believe her." She looked at me. "Do you?"

I shook my head.

"I'm not gonna wait a million years like that," I said. "I'm gonna start a new life soon."

"Me too. Some kinda way." She picked off another sliver of wood. "What do you want to do in your new life?"

"Make music."

She nodded. "Me too."

I tried a few notes of another song on my guitar. "You wanna practice 'Here Comes the Sun'?"

"Sure," she said. She cleared her throat and stood up. "I've sung it about five hundred times at home. My mom even sings along with me."

"Is she a good singer too?"

"No, she's the worst singer who ever lived."

We laughed.

"She says I got all my musical talent from my dad," said Heleena. "He was an opera singer in college, but now he just sells insurance in Oklahoma. I told him that I was starting a sort-of band. He said he'll come watch us perform. If we ever perform."

"I think I get all my musical talent from my dad too," I said.

Heleena cleared her throat again and sang notes for practice.

"Okay," she said. "Ready."

I got set for a D chord, but before I played anything, Heleena's face lit up like she'd had a brilliant realization.

"Hey, I just thought of something," she said. "We're doing it right now."

"We're doing what right now?"

"Making music."

"Oh." I looked down at my guitar. "You're right."

She nodded once and straightened her back. "Okay. Ready?"

"Yes," I said, still thinking about what she'd said. "I am."

★ ★ ★

The rain clouds were heavy, the sky grumbled, and it was getting dark by the time we finished rehearsing. Heleena's house was in the opposite direction from mine, so we walked to the corner together before going our own ways.

"That was fun," she said.

"Yeah." I looped my thumb around the guitar strap. "Maybe you can come over to my house sometime. Spend the night or something."

"That sounds great," she said. Her eyes brightened. "I'll listen to more Beatles music, and then I can tell you who my favorite is."

I held up my index finger. "Always pick George."

She laughed. "See you at school."

I started home slowly, thinking about our rehearsal. Even though it was getting dark, I wasn't ready to go back to Oak Park Drive, where I'd have to slip the guitar through my bedroom window before going inside. I could have kept practicing until the sun came up.

I was a little more than halfway home when the rain came. At first it was a few droplets. I picked up my pace and held the guitar tight against my back. In a few seconds, the sky cracked open and they weren't just little droplets anymore. Thunder roared. I broke into a run. My hair, clothes, and Chucks were soaked, but all I thought about was the guitar.

When I got home, there was no time to slip it through the window. I had to get inside right away. I was drenched from head to toe.

"Apple!" said my mom, when she saw me. I stood inside the doorway, dripping water all over the place. "I've been texting you for twenty minutes." She rushed off and came back with two towels. She put one under my feet. She started to wrap the other one around my shoulders, but then she saw the guitar.

"I was at the park with my friend Heleena," I said. I took the towel, dabbed my face, and wrapped it around my head. I wanted to get to my room right away to dry off the guitar, but my mother stood in front of me, eyeing it. She had a strange look on her face. Not anger exactly. Something else.

"Where did you get that?" she asked.

I didn't want to get Mr. Z in trouble, so I said, "I borrowed it from someone."

I waited for her to say something else, but she didn't.

"You should've answered my texts," she said. "Go change your clothes. Get dry before you get sick."

I stepped around her and dripped water all the way to my room. As I changed clothes I realized what was familiar about my mother's expression.

It was the remembering look.

28. Freedom

2FS4N: "I'll Follow the Sun"

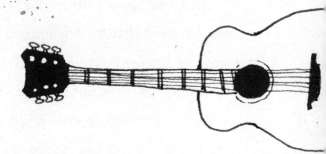

Even though it snowed in Chapel Spring the year we moved to America, I'd learned pretty quickly that the weather in south Louisiana isn't that much different from the Philippines. It's hot—really hot—and humid. Really humid. When you walk into an air-conditioned room, you immediately want to sit and rest and do nothing but feel the coolness. That's how hot it is, sometimes all the way through

December, but every once in a while there's a really amazing day. One of those days where there are white, puffy clouds floating through a bright blue sky, and even though the sun is out, it's not that hot, because the air is dry and there's a cool breeze coming from somewhere.

The Friday before the field trip was one of those days. I figured that by lunchtime it would be hotter than ever like usual, but at eleven o'clock it was still the amazing day it had been when I woke up.

Too bad we're stuck in school all day long, I thought.

I hooked my thumb under my guitar strap the same way I used to do with my purse and turned away from the brightness of the corridor and the loud, chatty seventh and eighth graders going outside for lunch.

Then I stopped. It took Heleena and Evan a few steps before they stopped too.

"What's the matter?" Evan asked. "Forget something?"

Kids bumped into me as I stood there frozen in place and looked back down the corridor.

My Jake Bevans radar was going off—he was coming toward us down the hall—but I still didn't move.

Forty-five minutes of freedom, I thought.

"Are you okay?" asked Heleena.

"Hey, it's the dog pound!" said Jake as he walked by with two of his friends. They barked a few times and continued on. I watched them go out the doors, into the bright sun.

"Let's go out on the quad today," I said.

"Good idea," said Evan, already stepping in that direction. "I need to find those bright yellow high-tops."

Heleena hesitated. "You two go." She looked at her feet. "I'm gonna finish up some homework in the library."

Evan was already drifting out of earshot.

"Come on, Heleena," I said. "It's an awesome day."

We always spent our lunch in the library or the band room. It was time to step into the daylight with the others.

Heleena looked like she wanted to protest again, but she didn't.

As we made our way outside I wondered if Alyssa would be standing by her usual tree, eating chips and gossiping, and if so I wondered who would be with her now.

I pointed to an empty spot on the grass.

"Let's sit there," I said.

I expected something to happen. I wasn't sure what, but not much did. Instead we just sat in the grass. Evan wandered around for a few minutes looking for Brian Watkins, then finally gave up and sprawled out next to us as we enjoyed the sun.

The sounds of the quad seemed louder than they'd ever been. Dozens of conversations, laughs at jokes I couldn't hear, boys shoving one another, sodas being opened, people walking around to find a place to sit. The quad felt like a foreign land, but here we were. Back in business.

"We should sit together on the bus," said Heleena. "Only if you want to." She put her hands in her lap. "But there's only two to a seat usually. So I can sit by myself. I don't mind. Or maybe on the way there, one of us can sit with someone else and on the way back we can switch. But I understand if you two would rather just sit together the whole time, since you're best friends."

The field trip. My city bus schedules were printed out and neatly tucked in my red notebook, inside my weekend backpack, under my bed. *On the way back*, Heleena had said. But I didn't plan on making the trip back.

Evan toed me with his shoe. "Quit zoning out."

I leaned back next to Evan and felt the warmth on my face. I squinted toward the clouds and watched a bird fly overhead. I wondered where it was going. I wondered if birds started new lives too.

Heleena also looked up. It was strange to see her sitting there, quiet and shy, with her hands in her lap. It was like she had a secret, but the kind of secret that needed to be shared. My mom used to say that once you said something out loud it became more true. I think that's why she always said "after what happened" instead of "after your dad died."

If that goes for the bad things, it must go for the good things too.

I sat up and brushed the grass off my hands. "Let's perform something," I heard myself say.

For a second I wondered if someone else had said it. Like Evan. But no, it was me. Every cell in my body hummed, but I picked up the guitar like it was nothing.

"Let's do what?" Heleena said.

"You remember. Our new life." I checked the strings. Who was I? My voice was cool and calm, but I was ready to burst out of my skin.

Evan's face lit up like a bulb.

I scanned the quad. Everyone was doing their usual thing. Just another day at lunch.

"What do you mean?" asked Heleena. Her eyes were two terrified circles.

"Let's do 'Here Comes the Sun.' Just like we did in the park."

Evan immediately jumped up. "This is gonna be epic."

I stood up too. But Heleena shook her head back and forth, back and forth. "There's no way I can do that in front of all these people." She scanned the quad. "I can't."

Evan chewed a nail and shifted from foot to foot.

I looked down at Heleena, who was shrinking into the grass. I motioned for her to stand up, but she was still shaking her head back and forth and rubbing her hands together like crazy.

"We sounded awesome in the park, right?" I said.

Her eyes darted around the crowd. "Yeah, but—"

"And we know 'Here Comes the Sun,' right?"

"Yes, but—"

I craned my head back and squinted. "And the sun is out."

"Okay, yeah, but—"

Evan chimed in. "And you're the best singer in the entire freaking universe, right?"

"Well, no, I don't think I'm—"

"Come on," I said, slipping the guitar strap over my head. I set up my fret hand. It was like I'd been possessed by someone else. "Everyone thinks we're freaks anyway. What difference does it make? Let's just start singing. It'll be fine. I swear. If people start laughing, we'll just play louder."

Possessed Apple was right. They already thought we were weirdos. And maybe we were. What's so wrong with that?

Evan didn't give Heleena any time to think it over. He clapped as loud as he could and hollered like he was at a concert and the main act had just stepped onstage. Eyes turned toward us. Some seemed confused, some irritated, and some amused. The more Evan hollered, the more kids quieted down and looked our way to see what was going on. Some of them looked like they were ready for a good laugh. That was the face Jake and his friends gave us, along with Alyssa, who was standing among them wearing more makeup than usual.

I wondered if Heleena would faint. She looked like she might. I couldn't blame her. Evan was cheering like a maniac, and he hadn't even waited for her to get ready.

But all eyes were on us now. We had to do something.

"I can't do it alone," I whispered to Heleena. "You're the voice. Come on." I glanced across the quad over all the eyes staring at us. Evan quieted down, and a few people laughed. I looked back at Heleena. "I'll sing backup."

At that she locked eyes with me.

"Okay," she said.

There was more laughter as she pulled herself to her feet.

Then there was only silence.

I adjusted my guitar. The tips of my toes and fingers tingled. I think my science teacher once said this kind of thing happened in a fight-or-flight response. Your body fills up with adrenaline and tries to figure out if it should run and hide or stay and fight.

I decided to stay and fight.

I counted off under my breath: four, three, two, one. Then I started playing. The sound seemed to fill the entire quad. I half expected Heleena to bolt, but then she opened her mouth and sang.

We'd practiced the song a dozen times under the red canopy in the park, but her voice was different here in front of all the people. She started off shaky, but so did I. At first I wasn't even sure I was hitting the right chords, and I didn't know if it sounded okay, because my ears were full of the sound of my heart beating. It must have though, because Heleena's voice evened out and strengthened. She sang louder, even though no one was laughing. My fingers cramped and ached from all the practicing I'd done since I'd borrowed the guitar, but I played through it. Sometimes, when you have pain, that's what you have to do—just keep playing until it goes away.

I got louder too.

The crowd stared and listened.

Even Evan didn't move. He'd never heard us play together.

And still, no one laughed.

When the song was over, we stopped playing and stood there like two mannequins. Unfortunately, Possessed Apple hadn't thought to come up with an encore plan. I didn't know what to do. Neither did Evan or Heleena. It was so quiet that I heard a bird chirp.

But then it wasn't so quiet anymore.

Someone cheered. Just one person. Loudly. Not making fun—a real cheer.

Gretchen.

She jumped up and down as if she were at an actual Beatles concert.

Other people did too. First Claire Hathaway. Then Danica Landry and Marie McCarron. Colby Matthews, Nick Preston, Elora Sullivan, Caleb Robinson. Then more, and more. They all gathered up in a big group around us. Brian Watkins was in the crowd too— when I saw him, I mouthed, *High-tops*, to Evan, and pointed him out. Evan gave a thumbs-up before his moppy head blended into the growing mob. Jake and Braden tried to throw a few barks our way, but they were drowned out by the applause. There were a million questions. Danica wanted to know where Heleena had learned to sing, and Marie asked why she never tried out for swing choir. Everyone wanted to look at my guitar. Even Alyssa.

"That was amazing, Apple," she said. "It reminded me of how we used to sing together in fifth grade. Remember?" Kids bumped into her, this way and that, all wanting to see if they could hold the guitar. "Maybe you could teach me to play and I could be in the group too."

She tried to say more, but the crowd swallowed her up, and she disappeared into it. I realized that's how she would always be: going where the crowd goes and then getting lost.

29. Ready

2FS4N: "Oh! Darling"

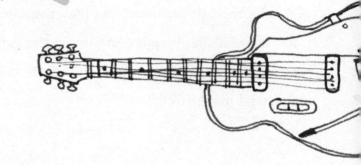

I had a performance buzz for the rest of the afternoon. It's weird how something can be so scary and awesome all at the same time. Heleena and I were the talk of the school. Especially Heleena. No one could believe her voice.

The buzz was still there when I got home. My mother was making her way to the yard with her garden gloves when I came through the door.

I was just about ready to tell her everything when she motioned to the guitar and said, "You need to return that to wherever you borrowed it."

"I don't have to. I get to keep it as long as I need."

"Yes, you do have to. Because I say."

I ignored her and decided to tell her about my day. And once I started talking, I couldn't stop.

"Today me and Heleena made our performance debut together in the quad at lunch. Everyone cheered for us. We sang 'Here Comes the Sun.' Do you know that song? Everyone loved it. It was so amazing, Mom. I can play other songs too. Like 'Blackbird,' which is my favorite, and 'Come Together.' I learned so fast, Mr. Z said I was a prodigy. He even asked if my dad was Jimi Hendrix. Can you believe that? I bet Dad was like Jimi Hendrix, probably. Was he, Mom? Was he good at guitar? I bet he was, wasn't he?"

She put up her hand. Her face was like stone.

"You sound like an American now, the way

you're talking to me," she said. "I said you need to give it back. So give it back. Tomorrow."

"No."

I saw the muscles in her jaw tighten. She tossed aside the garden gloves, took a step toward me, and put out her arm.

"Give it to me then," she said. "I'll return it to the school. I'll give it right to the principal."

She snapped her fingers and pointed at the guitar strap.

I pressed my lips together, tight. All the leftover good feelings from the afternoon morphed into something else, and I was ready to scream, cry, and explode all at once, right there in my mom's face. I yanked the guitar off my shoulder so hard that a sharp pain shot down my right arm. Then I shoved the neck into her open hand.

"Take it!" I said. "It doesn't matter. You know why? Because all I need is five more dollars, and I can buy one of my own. So you can bring it to school tomorrow, and I don't care!"

She pulled the guitar toward her. My body felt light now, without it on my back.

My eyes were wet. My skin was on fire. "Why do you hate music so much anyway? What kind of person doesn't like music? How could someone who loved the Beatles as much as Dad did be with someone who doesn't even have a favorite song?"

She set the guitar next to her and held it gingerly, like a cane.

"How did you know that your father liked the Beatles?"

"I'll show you." I stomped to my room, snatched *Abbey Road*, and walked back into the living room. Maybe she would try to take it away from me and throw it out, maybe she'd say it was from another life and I shouldn't have it, but I would take the chance. But even if she tried to destroy it—stomp on it, rip out the tape, burn it—it didn't really matter, because I would always be able to see my dad's name written in black marker, even if just in my mind. And *Abbey Road* would always belong to me, no matter what. Especially now.

My mom held the guitar with her right hand, so I pushed the tape into her left. She studied it. She ran her thumb across his name. "I told you to not take anything when we left."

"You took your Bible."

"That's different."

"How?"

"That Bible is mine." She looked up. Angry. "This doesn't belong to you."

"Maybe not before," I said. "Before, it belonged to my dad. His name was Herminio Yengko, and he listened to the tape so much that it's all cracked and worn down. He even wrote his name on it." The tears were here. I could feel them, warm on my face. "But that was before he died. Now it belongs to me. It's mine."

"It's not yours," she said.

"Fine! You can keep it too," I snapped. "I know all the songs anyway. And one day I'll play all of them! *Every single one!* And one day I'll write and play my own songs, and people'll write their names on *my* music, just like my father wrote his name there! So you can just *keep it, throw it away, or burn it* for all I care!" My voice kept getting louder and louder—a big, heavy rain cloud releasing all of its thunder. My mom wasn't ready. She didn't expect it. She looked at me with dark eyes. When I was done yelling, she stood there and let out a deep breath, like a deflated balloon. She hung her head. Her black hair fell around her face.

"Go to your room, Apple." Her voice was throaty and flat. "Go to your room and stay there."

It's hard for me to fall asleep when I'm mad, because the anger swirls around my head and keeps me awake like a bad song that won't stop playing. So I fell asleep later that night without any warning—on my rug with the lights on and my earbuds still in. When I opened my puffy eyes, Matt Costa was singing sunshine in my ear, even though it was pitch-dark outside my window and I had no idea how long I'd been asleep. My body ached from being on the floor. I stretched, long and hard. My head thumped the way it always does after a hard cry. And my stomach grumbled, because I'd missed dinner.

I took out the earbuds, yawned, and looked at the clock. It was almost midnight. My plan was to stay in my room until it was time for school, because I didn't want to look at my mother. I was too mad at her and regretted giving her Mr. Z's guitar. After all he'd done for me, I should've never put it in questionable hands. But I was hungry, and she was probably asleep anyway.

Matt Costa must have been louder than I thought, because I could still hear music playing. I reached down and turned it off. But it was still there.

I stood up and looked around.

It wasn't coming from my room.

But the only person on the other side of my door was my mother.

I opened my bedroom door and stepped out. "Mom?"

She had her legs tucked under her on the couch. My dad's tape was next to her on the cushion. She was holding Mr. Z's guitar. But not just holding it. *Playing* it. Quietly, like I'd done in my room all this time.

She didn't look surprised to see me, even though I probably looked more surprised than anyone in the history of surprises.

"Your father didn't write his name on that tape," she said. *"Sa akin."*

That means: "It was me."

"It was his favorite. He got it when he was a little boy, from an old *sari-sari* store. I was always worried it would get stolen or lost." She gently patted the guitar, like it was an old friend she hadn't seen in a long time. "He always wanted me to teach him some of the songs, but he was a terrible learner." She smiled. Her face softened. "After everything that happened . . ." She paused and started over. "I haven't played since he died. I wanted to leave it behind, so I wouldn't cry anymore. But I guess you never forget."

I swallowed. It felt like all the air was gone from my body.

"Mr. Z says it's like riding a bike," I said.

"I don't know," she said, chuckling. "I never learned how to ride a bike."

I laughed.

I could breathe again.

"He liked 'Oh! Darling.'" She looked up, eyes glistening. "But I liked 'You Never Give Me Your Money.' We had a joke about that one. I would say, 'You never give me your money,' and he would say, 'Oh, darling! That's because I don't have any.'" She laughed.

"I can play 'Oh! Darling,'" I said quietly.

"Okay, then." She lifted the guitar off her lap with both hands and handed it to me.

"I'm ready," she said.

When I was done, she gave me a tip.

Five dollars.

I also found out that my father's favorite Beatle was John.

And she told me what *atsara!* means.

Pickle.

The next morning I thought about that extra seat on the bus for the field trip. I decided I'd ask Gretchen if she wanted to sit with us. I also pulled all the New Orleans stuff out of my notebook and threw everything in the trash. Everything except Mr. Ted's itinerary.

And I wiped *Analyn* off my mirror.

Analyn is nice, but she doesn't make music.

30. Apple Yengko's IFs

I was born on an island in the Philippines.

I can play any Beatles song on the guitar.

My name is Apple.

Acknowledgments

Thank you to my family, especially Carolanne, who brings music to my life. Thank you, Jane Domino, Carolyn Jenks, Elora Sullivan, Davy DeGreeff, Janice Repka, Neil Connelly, Briana Woods-Conklin, Mary Kole, Sara Crowe, and everyone who supported Apple and her journey. Thank you, Fearless Fifteeners. Thanks to Justen Ahren and the Martha's Vineyard Writers Residency. Thanks to the entire Greenwillow team, especially Virginia Duncan, Lois Adams, and Sylvie Le Floc'h. And thank you, Jen. More than much.